RED RUSSIA

T. A. Thompson

Major Arcana

If it's in red, it's in Russian.

The Priestess

In the center of the action is Death. He appears as an oak red skeleton with a scythe. His bones are twisted in impossible directions and he is cutting a path through the waters of creation. He could best be described as running amok.

I am pleased to see him. It's the first time I have drawn the card and his location puts him at the heart of everything that is about to happen.

Honestly, I don't know why I do it: shuffle the cards right over left, cut the deck three times, and then think I can divine the future from the Tarot.

I call myself agnostic, but I'm more like an atheist; though admittedly, an atheist who pays respect to religion. I'm both a skeptic and an optimist, a cynic and an idealist. I rely on reason yet I am superstitious. It makes no sense, I know, but there it is nonetheless.

The Death card is welcome because Death signifies change. Here in the center it means nothing will be spared. Change is going to affect the past, which is revealed in the two cards to the right. It will influence the future, which lies in the cards to the left. There will be alterations in the subconscious mind which can be seen in the cards just below Death, and above Death is the conscious mind with its goals and aspirations.

All of it is going to end. A major event is on the horizon.

The immediate past is the Four of Coins. I have come to resent this card. It is stability. It is financial certainty. It is the starter mansion in the suburbs, 401(k), hedge funds, life insurance, and the threat of procreation which will result in school runs, crayon art, and an abrupt end to sexy Halloween.

Beside the Four of Coins is the Prince of Coins. This is the bastard responsible for all the high-walled private-gated security. God, he is boring. All the Coins are, but the Prince is particularly tedious. Not yet a king, he is always striving upward, forever seeking new wealth, greater conquests, proving his worth by adding new stones to his fortress, as though the thick walls of prosperity might make him invulnerable.

The Prince has forgotten that Death has no time to lay siege. Death doesn't recognize walls or wealth or fancy titles like prince, president, or CEO. Death has his own agenda, and Death is going to ensure we won't have to deal with the Prince of Coins for much longer.

The Prince is going to be surprised to learn his fortress is not as stable as he thinks. Discontent has been working at the foundation for some time. You can see it in the subconscious. There's a dark pit of hell forming in the cellar. The Ten of Wands sits beside the Seven of Swords: every attempt to escape has been suppressed; every action is futile. The situation down below is dire.

The conscious mind wants to be free of the oppression, and the presence of the Queen of Swords indicates freedom may be gained through violence. This queen is prone to cut people's heads off. Of all the women you don't want to cross, it's her. The solution to every crisis is a swift execution. Her weapon of choice is a sword, but beside her is the Two of Wands. Things are going to get messy. The wands are clubs, blunt weapons that bludgeon and crush, and it is with this primitive instrument she will act.

To the left of Death is the future. The cards are the Devil and the Moon.

The deck holds such cards as the Lovers and Lust, but no card is more sensual than the Devil. In the Crowley deck, he appears as the god Pan. Behind him is a phallus that rises majestically up until it pierces heaven. There is no sin in the Devil. He is not evil. What he signifies in the Tarot is carnal energy at its purest.

The Devil alone is nothing to fear, but each card in a spread is defined by the card beside it. If you see the Tower and the Sun together, it means someone is going to die, but pair the Sun with any ace and it's the start of something marvelous. Find the Lovers with the Nine of Swords and you can expect a divorce, but the Nine of Swords beside the Ten of Wands is rape.

To discover the Devil and Death in the same spread is momentous. But the Devil paired with the Moon speaks of dark deeds. It foreshadows secrets, depravity, and midnight treachery.

That the two of them have been set loose by Death is nothing short of sinister.

The Empress

The Prince of Coins is coming home early from work. He doesn't know I call him such, and honestly he'd be insulted because he thinks he's the king.

Sure, a man's home is his castle, but if he shares it with a woman, he knows his rule is limited.

I reign in this castle, this architecturally ambiguous behemoth that sits large among similar monstrosities in the River Run gated community. One more ring on my finger and it will be mine legally. I already wear the contract: a four carat square diamond set in platinum. Four carats and four sides, the symbolism is rife, but the Prince of Coins doesn't see it.

I see it though. I know four plus four equals eight, and eight is not a number you want to base a marriage on. Four is stability, but eight is trouble.

I don't really believe any of this, but still I know it. And in knowing it, there is the risk of a self-fulfilling prophecy.

It's the fault of my parents: new age hippies. I spent my youth traveling the circuit of never ending Renaissance fairs. My mother read palms. My father made candles. We lived like gypsies in a caravan. It wasn't quite the circus, but it was tragically close.

I know a dozen ways to tell your fortune: tea leaves, I Ching, Tarot, crystal balls, the palm of your hand, the feel of your skull, commune with the dead, Ouija board, table tapping, numerology, astrology, and good old psychic intuition.

The things I know... God, it's embarrassing. So are my parents. My fiancé hasn't met them yet. I'm hiding them lest he figure out I'm trailer trash. I need to seal the deal before he

9

learns too much. To make this relationship work, I've had to keep some fairly important things hidden, including my cards.

He's not yet seen himself represented in a spread. He doesn't know he's an archetype, the Prince of Coins incarnate.

To his face, I call him Peter. I call him darling and dear, and sometimes in bed I call him a rebel because he likes it, but he's not.

He's stable.

He aspires to greatness.

He wants to dig a wine cellar.

Well, he wants to contract labor to dig a wine cellar, but regardless, he wants one beneath this atrocity of suburban conformity.

I don't know why I did it, but I tricked him once. I poured a twelve-dollar merlot into a hundred-dollar zinfandel and served it with dinner. After studying the label and spotting the price, he confirmed it was excellent.

I never let him in on the joke, mostly because it wasn't funny, but also for fear of giving him ideas. If he ever looks past my designer labels, he might recognize me for an imposter as well.

He has a master's degree in economics from Cornell. I have one in Russian literature from UConn. His degree produces tangible assets, while mine... Well, there's really nothing you can do with a degree in Russian literature except bore the shit out of people at dinner.

But corporate executives don't want wives that compete financially. They want wives who look pretty and act smart. No one needs to learn my GPA was 2.4. I speak Russian and read the classics. In the world of MBAs, that makes me a bona fide intellectual.

And Peter, well, Peter is considered the next Morris, which is something when he works for Morris & Hugo Enterprise. Senior management at M&H calls him "the kid." It's not just that he'll be thirty on his next birthday, but he has an Xbox in his office. In his emails, he refers to the board of directors as team-killing noobs. He encourages map hacking the competition, and he gives TL;DR summations. The junior staff thinks he's awesome. They think he's hip and edgy. But what do they know? They all majored in business.

And business right now is Russian timber. That Peter has a fiancée who speaks the language and, further, can bore the shit out of the Russian elite with their own literary giants, well, that pretty much guarantees Peter is the new tsar of the lumber account. He just needs to seal the deal and make me his wife.

Not only will he score a pay raise, he'll win an apartment in Moscow and another in London.

High-fucking-five.

He can't believe his fortune, but then he's not looking at the same one I am.

He's driving home to collect me and then we're off to the airport and our first visit with the Russian executives of Konstantin Imperiya. Peter has to charm them into signing a contract before he's offered control of the timber account.

And no one doubts the Russians will sign because, at this point, closing the deal is all down to the power of personal relationships. And who doesn't love Peter? He's awesome! He's perfect! And his fiancée speaks Russian, you know?

Together, we're the company's most apt and adorable couple.

I even taught Peter to say "Ya ne govoryu po-ruski, no my smozhem govorit cherez moyu zhenu." I do not speak Russian, but we will be able to talk through my wife.

I didn't need to study business to understand the economy of value.

I need to make myself irreplaceable before Peter learns I have a couple of crazy parents in a trailer park, a Tarot deck in my carry-on, and an addiction to sleeping pills. Yes, well, I didn't mention it because we hardly knew each other two pages ago.

Let's see, at this point I take zopiclone, Ambien, methaqualone, and promethazine. Half the cocktail gets me to sleep and the other half keeps me there, otherwise a person might wake up in the grocery store parking lot trying to start a stranger's car with the keys to their secret P.O. Box.

Yes, well, never mind that either, because after the trip to Russia, and after the wedding, I won't need a P.O. Box because I'm going to cut back to just one pill, which a real US doctor will prescribe and a real US pharmacy will fill, and then I'll introduce Peter to my parents.

And then everything will be honest between us because I really do lov... I mean, I really do like... uh... *need?* him. Whatever. He's a great guy. Look at him, coming in from the city with a Zegna briefcase in one hand and in the other he's thumbing through a Mobiado phone, talking loud and bombastic to god knows who on the headset hidden in his ear.

He works hard.

He provides without resentment.

He's given me everything the trailer-trash child in my soul ever wanted.

Good Lord, I can be such a fool. I need to put these cards away and stop thinking they can predict the future.

*　*　*

Peter comes through the front door still talking. "Me and Sibyl are meeting them offline tomorrow. By the close of play, I'll have us in bed with Konstantin himself."

He drops his briefcase just inside the door so it rests against the bags I've packed. He gives me an appreciative thumbs-up and then adjusts his headset to respond, "If the timber industry was scalable, every venture pig on the big board would be looking to fill their plate, but we're vertical in this field."

Don't be alarmed. When corporate executives get really excited, they leverage their learnings against comprehension to revolutionize English.

He strides across the quartz floor to embrace my waist while assuring the person on the phone, "Not a worry. I've got my own Russian sharpshooter. Sibyl's a regular Wookiee in the hills. She'll snipe 'em dead." And then squeezing me to his chest, he asks, *"Amirite?"*

If we're going to get through this, just do like I do: nod and smile.

Releasing me, he walks to the refrigerator and pulls an H2Yo bottle from the shelf. M&H Enterprise is funding the H2Yo venture and marketing the water to young urban blacks. Don't laugh like I did because irony isn't part of the pitch.

13

From this insular culture, Peter speaks to his kin, "I haven't been over the wall in months," meaning he hasn't worked with anyone outside M&H Enterprise. "The Muppets have kept me on the mothership doing hotshots for weeks." I have no idea what that means, but Peter is glad it's over. He starts singing, "They say you gotta toe the line, they want the water not the wine, but when I see the signs, I jump on that lightning bolt."

And I am so unhip, so uncool and uninformed, I have no idea what that's about either.

He ends the call by saying, "We'll circle back later this week for some PvP."

To me he growls, "We've got time for some PvP too." Player versus player, and he's not talking Xbox like before.

I am not so unaware as not to recognize Peter is a highly desirable catch. Never mind his linguistic artifices, he is actually capable of conversing in generally recognizable phrases, and he's considerate, intelligent, not prone to violence, public scenes, or any greater vice than vanity. He goes to the gym, uses more grooming products than me, and while he only buys designer labels, he also makes them look good. Sure, he can't tell a merlot from a zinfandel, or Salinger from Steinbeck, but he knows the difference between bonds and equities and when to purchase each. He knows how to make friends, promote his own goals, and destroy the competition. With his skills, attributes, and inventory, he's the perfect hero, an honest-to-god Prince of Coins incarnate that any woman should be happy to find in her future, and yet (Isn't there always a great deal of flattery before the word that inevitably undoes everything that precedes it?), I am unmoved.

He growls for sex, but I am bored.

14

I don't need the Tarot, a crystal ball, or my psychic third eye to predict every sound and every move that will ensue. It's all so routine.

I wish he had a kink. But after digging through his online porn habits, I'm fairly certain he doesn't. It was straight-up guy-on-girl action, a blowjob and a fuck.

One look at Mirra Lokhvitskaya and you'll see more passion in a nineteenth-century poet than the conservative side of PornHub.

I try to make sex with Peter more exciting. I talk, I resist, I submit or take control, but whatever I do, I'm still told to quiet down and go slow, or worse, be normal.

Normal.

It is what I've strived for. It's the facade I've contrived. But normal is truly and thoroughly dull.

And so I say to Peter, "I wish we could, but we really don't have time."

It's a lie because we have electronic tickets, priority check-in, and are pre-checked with the TSA.

Peter's idea of normal doesn't include standing in lines. It's the way he was raised. His mother was a tenacious social climber who fought her way onto Connecticut's Gold Coast. To her, image is everything. If she knew her most precious darling little Peter were engaged to a girl who had been raised in a camper, she'd explode in such a way that the wedding registry at Tiffany's would shower silver shrapnel all over the select guests at the Hartford Club.

In my Tarot deck, she is represented by the card Justice, and she always appears in a spread with the Ace of Swords, which makes her scary as hell.

One day she's going to learn my parents haven't been touring the Samoan Islands on a philanthropy mission, and that's the day her sword will cut a divide between Peter and me.

That is if Death doesn't do it first.

Art

Money for the privileged is a social construct, while for the less fortunate, it's a work contract, and the agreement is a curious one when you've spent most of your life without either.

Take for instance two first-class tickets to Moscow. Care to guess how much they cost?

Before you waste any time searching the web for the answer, let me warn you that first class isn't an option on the big fare finders. If you're the sort to search the web for a ticket, they know you're not interested in first class.

So take your guess: two first-class round-trip tickets from New York to Moscow.

Peak tourist season: June.

Traveling time each way: ten hours.

If you booked ahead and got it for a deal, it's only two thousand dollars per hour, or a steal at forty thousand.

There's not a trailer-trash child alive who doesn't know that's a double wide.

That could be home.

But for the elite, it's a place to sit for ten hours.

For M&H Enterprise, it's considered a necessary expense. In this business, presentation is all important. And while you might think no one would know, or even care to know, the specifics of our travel arrangements, in this case you'd be as wrong as I originally was. The Russian consultant hired by M&H to prepare us for this trip went to some lengths to explain that every part of our arrival, our stay, and our departure will be known to the executives of Konstantin

Imperiya, because Konstantin Imperiya's executives are siloviki.

There's no English equivalent for silovik. It doesn't translate succinctly because to create something as Machiavellian as a silovik requires both the KGB and the GRU, and then a shift from communism to capitalism followed by a gear-grinding reverse into despotism.

Konstantin himself isn't silovik; he's Bratva. Bratva is easy. Bratva means brother, specifically brothers in crime, also known incorrectly as the Russian Mafia. Calling something as wholly unique as the Bratva by the name Russian Mafia is like writing off the siloviki as corporate spies.

M&H Enterprise has corporate spies, but Konstantin Imperiya has siloviki. Siloviki are members of the secret security forces. They're officers of the former KGB, GRU, FSB, and SVR, which are essentially all acronyms for spies, spooks, shadows, and assassins.

For the siloviki, business and Russia are the same corporate state for which they remain spies, spooks, shadows, and assassins.

The hired consultant taught us another word too: kompromat.

Now this one is fun. To a room full of M&H executives, the consultant said, "As soon as you opened dialogue with Konstantin Imperiya, they would have started compiling dossiers on each of you. That they've agreed to talk means they have enough compromising material to blackmail. At this point, if you fail to give them what they want, they will release this kompromat to the media. If you want to keep your secrets, I'd advise you to stay home."

And Hugo, of Morris & Hugo Enterprise, had laughed. "That's why we're sending the kid," he said. "Peter's too young to have done anything serious."

I'm not really worried because sleeping pills and hippy parents are too insignificant to register on the mental radar of a scheming silovik or a murdering Bratva, and Peter is a four-sided Prince of Coins, too stable to have ever done anything exciting enough to be worthy of a kompromat.

In the first-class cabin of British Airways, Peter's only concern is the daisy chain of electronic devices he's recharging through both our power outlets and the delay associated with satellite Wi-Fi over the Atlantic.

Because Peter doesn't want to be called a lagging feeder, he can't PvP, so he's left with few other options than talking with me.

Compiling dossiers on potential business partners is not something exclusive to Konstantin Imperiya, or the siloviki. The Competitive Intelligence Department of M&H provided Peter with every known detail they could find, steal, or buy on the executives and founder of Konstantin Imperiya. Peter could repeat it verbatim two weeks ago, but he reads it again to me.

"Maksim Volikov, Deputy Chief of Konstantin Imperiya and second largest shareholder. Born November ninth, nineteen sixty-six. Graduate of law from Saint Petersburg's Leningrad University."

I glean from this a lot more than Peter. The totals are present in my mind without effort or attempt. First is numerology: Volikov is a six. Next is astrology, which marks Volikov as a Scorpio, and then the Chinese Zodiac calls him a Snake. Accepted western symbolism would suggest he's poison, but making him significantly more dangerous are the

19

double 6 and double 9 clearly visible in his date of birth; they signify he's a master of duplicity. Don't bother wondering if he's Yin or Yang, black or white, good or evil, because try all you like to trip up a double 6 and 9 and they will merely stand on their head and insist they were the other all along. I could devolve even further into the occult and really make Volikov out to be a monster, but in that way lies madness, and so, as not to appear insane, I share none of this with Peter.

Instead, Peter shares his psychosis with me. "In the organogram, Maksim so saksim makes Saks look SIM."

I won't argue any part of that because I barely recognize half the words as English. Never mind though, Peter is pressing on me a tablet still attached to the charger. "Cognisize this." He leans into my lap to tap open a page in the intelligence report.

It reads: During the 1994 takeover of Steellyov, Maksim Volikov was believed to have used his FSB position to coerce shareholders to accept less than market value for stocks. Several board members were arrested for tax evasion during the acquisition, and though it was ruled a suicide, the CEO of Steellyov was found asphyxiated in his car. The takeover was financed with high yield bonds sold to the public through a Moscow bank in which Volikov's relatives were partners. Shortly after the company was acquired, it was dissolved for assets and the bank closed as bankrupt.

"Good lord."

As though I had laughed, Peter says, "That's not the funny part," and leans in again to scroll down the screen.

The last sentence reads: Fear of reprisals from Volikov and his supporters in the FSB ensured no investigation followed.

Peter smiles and winks. "That's an anecgloat if I've ever heard one."

"Anecgloat?"

"You know, like an anecdote for the ego." He shakes his head in dismay and says, "Man, you are acluistic." I'll never know exactly what it is that I am because next Peter says, "This whole business with the FSB, like *woo~ooo~ooo.*" He throws his hands up in mock fear and makes ghost sounds. "The *scary* FSB, it's just a cover image. But it's prime target for some serious impression management."

Impression management? I can't ask again, so I just look confused.

Peter explains, "Window licking." But as that doesn't change my expression, he further clarifies, "Big up. Cater out. Soft soap. *No?* Flattery, Sibyl. Simple flattery. Is that so hard to understand?"

Well, not when you use consumer-ready words. But I don't say this.

And anyway, he's moved on. Reading once more from the dossier, he says, "Isaak Madulin, third largest shareholder in Konstantin Imperiya and Chief Financial Officer. Mayor of Bereznik and former director of the Bereznik sawmill. Born March thirteen, nineteen sixty-two, he's a graduate of law from Saint Petersburg State University."

He's a nervous Pisces with a Chinese Tiger fishing his waters. The symbolism infers he may be inclined to suicide or other forms of self-harm, but more significant, being ruled by the number seven indicates, rather specifically, that this worried Pisces spends his earnings on either very debauched women or opiates.

I ask, "Is he married?"

"Going on twenty years. Also has two daughters and a son."

"Mistress?"

"Are you kidding? Look at the guy." Peter taps open an image of a man with thinning hair, heavy-lidded eyes, and a joyless expression that matches his business gray suit. Peter's diagnosis: "Dead inside."

"He's four years younger than Volikov but looks as old as Konstanin."

"If that crypt walker is getting flesh and I'm gettin..." Then Peter remembers it's me, not one of the junior execs, and stops himself. To get distance from the awkwardness, he looks to the widescreen over the liquor cabinet and watches the animation of the plane flying north along the Atlantic coast. He complains, "It hasn't moved in an hour."

I have to smile because we've only been in the air forty minutes and the first he saw the animation was ten minutes ago.

To help him focus, I say, "Tell me about Konstantin."

"The kingpin: Konstantin Zomanov, born July twenty-three, nineteen fifty."

Even the most casual fortune-teller will recognize Volikov is interesting, but Konstantin is downright astounding.

Numerology has Konstantin as a nine. Astrology says he's a Leo and the Chinese Zodiac names him a Tiger. Accepted Western symbolism would infer he's a cat with nine lives, but making him fabulously portentous is again the date of birth: July 23. Whole books have been dedicated to the number twenty-three, and July 23 in particular.

Peter says, *"Kawinkydink:* that's the date you set for our wedding."

Not a kawinkydink. And also, probably not a wise date to start a marriage. Well, at least, not if you're the sort to believe in such things.

If you've not read any of the books dedicated to the topic, here's the TL;DR: July 23 is the day the universe took acid, tripped balls, and birthed Eris, the Goddess of Discordia. Her birthday, as is Konstantin's, is the day of chaos. It's the anniversary of everything surreal.

For all it might imply about me and what I hope from our marriage, the significance of this date is also not the sort of thing I'm inclined to share with Peter.

Instead, I let him continue reading. "Konstantin was first arrested at ten, left school later the same year, and then, five arrests later at the age of fifteen, he's sentenced to forced labor at Dalstroy Gulag." Peter turns in his seat to look at me with confusion. "How does a guy that spent over two decades in prison come out and rule a kingdom the size of Texas?"

If we were talking about an American tycoon, the answer would be family money, but as Peter says, "The little bastard came from Latvian peasant stock. He was raised in an orphanage, for Christ's sake. The man racked up twenty-three years going in and out of the gulag, and now he's a logging magnate? Explain that."

I could expound upon July 23, or the 23 Enigma, or say *two plus three equals five* and it's the Law of Fives, but that's all far too esoteric, and besides, the intelligence dossier has explained it better, so I simply lean into Peter's seat and run my finger over the tablet so it highlights the three words: thief in law.

"Thief in law," Peter scoffs. "Prison thieves don't control a billion dollars in raw resource."

But I know better because the moment I heard the phrase *thief in law,* I went slightly dotty with infatuation. While Peter was memorizing the chief executives' biographies, I was absorbing every detail Google could find about this uniquely Russian prison phenomenon.

If you've ever amused yourself in a role-playing fantasy game with a faction of thieves and a Thieves Guild, you've essentially seen the thieves in law as they operate from Russia's prisons. They're a criminal fraternity with a strict code of ethics, rituals, and expectations. Break the rules and an honest-to-god council of thieves will decide your fate, and a devote hierarchy will enforce it.

While it is crime organized, it is not organized crime, though the two intersect.

There are some codes of conduct that set a thief in law apart from the Bratva. A thief in law cannot have a legitimate job or make money honestly, and they are bound to help their criminal kin over blood relatives. Falling out of favor but still held sacred by many, a thief in law cannot marry or have children, and they cannot own property or consider any place home other than prison.

Russian organized crime draws many of its members from the thieves in law, and for that, Russian organized crime is far more loyal than the Mafia ever dreamed of being, partly because the Bratva are recruited in prison and have already proven they can and will go to jail, and the thief in law doesn't get crowned a vor, thief, until he's been jailed repeatedly and demonstrated he won't cooperate with the authorities.

The Bratva want thieves in law within their ranks because it gives them credibility. And the thieves in law join the Bratva because they get due respect.

That Konstantin is both the Pakhan—the boss, the godfather, the don—of the Zomanov Bratva and also a thief in law pretty much makes him a king of thieves and that the siloviki obey his command makes him terrifyingly powerful.

He sits at the head of a table that feeds not only spies, spooks, and assassins from the government, but also burglars, swindlers, and hit men from the prisons, and dining beside them are police, civil servants, and judges from the public services, and finally there's a whole host of politicians toasting his health with wine stolen from the church and anointed holy by the priest at his side.

Konstantin is an exemplary, though not entirely unique, Russian oligarch. Sure, he controls a vast forest, but another Bratva just like him controls most of the steel, and another has a monopoly on gas. There are Bratva in gold, oil, and diamonds, and most of them own a bank or two. And they are all, each and every one of them, a thief in law.

I try to explain this to Peter, but he stops me by enunciating loudly, "T. B. I." After affirming the *traumatic brain injury* I've caused him, he declares, "I didn't ask to drink from the fire hose."

Hand to his head, Peter squeezes his temples.

I ask, "Have you got a headache as well?"

And he grumbles an agreement.

I don't have a headache, but with nine hours remaining in this flight, I think it's time to drown our minds for real.

Because zopiclone and methaqualone aren't prescribed in the US, I keep one in an aspirin bottle and the other mixed up in a bottle of Tylenol. They look similar, but the desperate eye of an addict can tell them apart. Ambien is perfectly legal, but Peter has read the stories of people wandering around after midnight whacked out of their minds, roasting marshmallows over Zippos and burning down the house, or driving to The Met in their underwear, and, of course, there was our neighbor who decorated his front lawn with Christmas lights in June. All very embarrassing. To Peter, Ambien is nothing short of evil and he won't allow it in the house, so the Ambien is with the methaqualone pretending to be Tylenol as well. Promethazine is the magic pill that will prevent these mad nocturnal walkabouts, but as I don't have a prescription for that either, it's in a Benadryl bottle.

Because half of what I need to get me through the night isn't exactly legal, I just go ahead and get everything online. When it comes to pop culture and most things current, I'm truly passé, but I know all about Tor, Valhalla, Silk Road and the Dread Pirate Roberts, god bless every one of his incarnations.

Peter's wallet is Brioni and mine is BitCoin. That's another secret I'll have to dispose of after Russia and the wedding, and dropping back to one pill, closing my P.O. Box, and pulling my parents out of hiding. I might need to make a list.

Just thinking about it is more than I can really cope with.

I give Peter half a tablet from the aspirin bottle and I take two from the Tylenol.

He asks, "Why are you taking two of that and I'm only taking *half* of this if we both have a headache?"

26

"Mine's worse," I explain. And then smiling, *"Trust me. I always take care of you."* I kiss his cheek and assure him, "If you're not better in thirty minutes, I'll give you two of these."

But that will never happen. I've spent years building up a resistance to every hypnotic on the market. I can mix methaqualone with Ambien and still make more sense than Peter on a conference call. The half zopiclone I give Peter will either put him to sleep or make it so he doesn't care if the little plane moves across the map.

And, as expected, twenty minutes later he's dead to the extravagances of first class, and he won't appreciate anything again until we land in Moscow.

The Sun

By the time we clear Immigration, it's 5:00 a.m. and the summer sun is already shining bright through the vast expanse of glass that fronts Moscow's Domodedovo terminal.

Peter looks at the sun, then at his watch, and back to the sun again. *"What the fuck?"* He curses the airline, "Goddamn military time. Why couldn't the captain just give the time in normal hours?"

I want to explain that zero-five-hundred really is 5:00 a.m. and that Russia is simply in the long days of the White Nights when the sun is only below the horizon for a few short hours, but the terminal is loud with people and I'd have to shout to be heard. And anyway, Peter doesn't think he has time for an explanation. He's got morning meetings, and by all appearances, it's 9:00 a.m.

Nearer the exit, he finds the line of drivers holding whiteboards, and on one of them, his name is scrawled. Striding purposefully forward, his face still showing fury the airline provided the incorrect time, Peter points with aggressive urgency at the man and then gestures to himself and next jabs his finger toward the doors leading out, indicating he will lead and the driver should follow, as though he knows where the car is.

Cultural mistake #1: Don't point at a Russian. Actually, don't point at anyone, but especially don't point at a Russian. Where the Japanese will silently register the offense and then make you pay for it later in negotiations, a Russian will throw down the placard with your name, raise his fist to shove his thumb between the middle and index finger, and shout, "Kurite moju trubku, pedik!"

Because Peter is forcing his way through the early morning crowd, he doesn't see or hear the insults.

I do, though.

And I know the hand gesture means fuck you, and "kurite moju trubku" means suck my cock, while "pedik" is a very specific prison term for a man that's been made the blockhouse bitch.

As the average Russian businessman has no need to unnecessarily humble his closest employee, and the Bratva would never belittle a brother, the driver is not dressed in a demeaning black tux and cap but is instead in a skin tight T-shirt that reveals not only his hard physique but also the horns of a bull tattooed below his neck.

Entering the stream of departing passengers, the driver shouts, "Idi syuda, blyad," or, in English, Come here, motherfucker, and pushes after Peter.

We've been on Russian soil for approximately thirty minutes and Peter is about to have his first fight.

Never mind that Peter has never before *been* in a fight, what's following is such a dangerous beast he's been marked with ink as a warning, so there's absolutely no chance Peter might win.

I don't need to be an expert on prison tats to understand what the bull means. I read the Tarot, and the bull is an archetype; the bull transcends cultures.

It's already evident that the man charging Peter is an aggressive and easily riled creature, and being an animal of honor, the bull is quickly provoked by the red cape of disrespect, which Peter unwittingly snapped in his direction, but the symbolism that concerns me most is the blood dripping from the horns, because that surely signifies this animal is inclined to gore/shiv his antagonizers.

Because Konstantin is Bratva, it's safe to assume the driver is as well, and you do *not* disrespect a Bratva, especially not in front of his brothers, or when anyone is looking. And, at this point, everyone is looking.

Peter is still marching fast steps for the exit, and the only reason the driver hasn't caught him is because he's shouting such crude obscenities people are stopping in his path to gawk, whereupon they are immediately trampled.

First to fall is a small Asian with a pastry, and next down is young woman filming with her phone. The driver jumps over a child in a stroller and then shoves an orthodox priest into a trolley of luggage. A babushka in winter wool takes offense at the ruckus and swings a plastic bag made heavy and round with a cabbage at the driver's head, but he dodges and ducks, so momentum spins her around and throws her to the floor as well.

Behind Peter screams erupt and further insults are thrown, but as none of it is in English, Peter is oblivious to it all.

Standing near the central information desk are four officers, and this gives me a moment's hope, but the police look at the driver, then out the glass front of the terminal, and whatever they see out there makes them tut and cluck and then, as not to bear witness to what's about to unfold, they move off into the depths of the airport and disappear.

The only thing I can imagine to be worse than one angry Bratva is a whole mess of angry Bratva, so I quickly wade through the pandemonium to follow. I make the priest decent again by brushing down his cassock and say, "Izvinitye," Sorry, then kick the cabbage back to the babushka and say, "Izvinitye," again. I avoid the Asian going mental over

31

his pastry, and by the time I make it to the newly injured backpacker with the broken finger, Peter has made it outside.

Moments later, the driver and I clear the sliding doors together. I'm about to start apologizing in earnest, but ahead, on the wide expanse of pedestrian pavement, is an ostentatious convoy of cars, and my attention is momentarily diverted—no, my attention is actually smacked backward and dazed—by the unabashed vulgarity of the Russian nouveau riche.

The metallic gold Land Rover would stand out as magnificently garish if it weren't for the faux marble Maserati, the stretch six-door Jaguar, and the pinstriped Bentley lowrider, but making the cars look practically ordinary is the collection of men smoking cigarettes beside the four-foot tires of a Mercedes Unimog draped in camouflage net.

I do realize Peter is about to lose his life, and now is really not the time to judge, but I can't help wondering who let these men out of the house dressed as they are, and also, just who did what to their hair? I'm fairly certain one has dipped his head in a bucket of high-gloss polyurethane and then styled and dried it to achieve the rippling waves of a plastic Ken doll, and another has somehow managed to achieve the look of upholstery tassels across his forehead. There's a convincing version of Sid Vicious—shirtless, rib bones bulging across his skinny ivory-white chest—and next to him is an Elvis, a James Dean, and a fat Johnny Rotten. There's a blond with cornrows and a Mongolian with a mohawk, but what stops me stupid is the taxidermied head of a polar bear another is using for a hat.

The bald one would look almost normal if not for the velvet smoking jacket and Armani slippers, and while there's nothing wrong with a crew cut, the owner of that style is decked out top to bottom in clashing Louis Vuitton symbols so he looks like a set of mismatched luggage.

Not one of these outlandish individuals is in the dossier provided by M&H intelligence, but it is to these men the driver is shouting, "I am going to kill this *khueplet*," which, given the limitations of Pushkin and Tolstoy, I can only manage to roughly translate as dick weaver.

Upon hearing this threat, I reflexively grab the driver's shoulder and then immediately regret it, but before he can fully twist my wrist and flip me to the ground, the fine gentleman in the smoking jacket barks, "Ostyn!" Chill! as in Chill the hell out, and the polar bear growls, "Krissha poyekhala?" Have you lost your mind?

From the back of the stretch Jaguar, a familiar face emerges. Maksim Volikov, Deputy Chief of Konstantin Imperiya, is immediately recognizable from the intelligence report. Dressed in a modest gray suit, he has a bureaucratic appearance that might lead a spectator to believe he is the accountant for this circus, but Peter knows Volikov is the most powerful silovik in the firm.

Still completely clueless to the chaos of his first blunder, Peter throws a hand up in recognition and beams widely while calling, "Maksim, my man. It's either later than I think, or Chernobyl is lighting up the sky."

Cultural mistakes #2 and #3: Don't smile at a Russian and don't joke about Chernobyl.

Not making light of a national disaster is self-explanatory, but the issue around smiling is rather more complicated. During the Cold War, Americans were painted as particularly insincere and devious, and this was evidenced by our ever-present gratuitous smile. Capitalism and greed was to blame for much of it. The least culpable were fast-food

33

employees coerced into disingenuous exchanges, but fully accountable was the smooth-talking American salesman and the ultimate leering conman, Uncle Sam.

TL;DR: In Russia, unwarranted smiles mark a person as either a hustler or an imbecile.

And as Peter and I are the only ones in hearing distance to speak English, all the Russians know is some fool is grinning about a nuclear meltdown.

He looks to be an idiot.

Disapproval has made Volikov's features cold, but he walks forward to shake Peter's hand and say, "Dobroye utro. Meenya zavoot Maksim Volikov. Vy govorite po-ruski?"

The American smile on Peter's face broadens in alarm and then, exactly as I taught him, but with entirely too much enthusiasm and an unexpected Jewish accent, he exclaims, "Ya ne govoryu po-RUSKI! No my smozhem govorit cherez MOYI ZHENU!" I do not speak RUSSIAN! But we will be able to talk through MY WIFE!

And in Russian, the driver demands of me, "You married this *pizda s ušami?*"

Struggling to interpret pizda s ušami, I answer in Russian "Not yet," which makes a few people chuckle because it seems like I'm agreeing to the part where Peter is a cunt with ears.

The driver asks, "But you plan to marry the cunt with ears?"

Denying Peter is any such thing, I snap, "Nyet."

But this just allows the driver to ask with provocative hope, "Nyet?"

So I correct, "Da," and while most of them laugh, I correct again, "Nyet."

34

Finally, Volikov tells him, "Zakroy rot." Shut your mouth.

With an expression that could win over a judge in a beauty pageant, Peter looks back to me and asks through his teeth, *"What's happening?"*

I explain, "We're having a slight cultural misunderstanding. It might get better if you stopped smiling."

Peter abruptly appears somber. He looks the group over and then, relaxing his shoulders, he audibly exhales.

And I am endlessly thankful. The shift in Peter's demeanor means he is fully focused and about to fix this shit, because this is what Peter does best: he fixes shit.

He says, "Mr. Volikov, it's über cool to finally interface with you. Let me introduce my fiancée, Sibyl."

And I walk forward to translate, changing *über cool* to *very good* and *interface* to *meet*.

Reaching for Volikov's hand again, Peter grasps it with sincerity to explain, "We weren't expecting such a rad reception. I can't tell you how amped I am to find you—*the big enchilada*—here."

I change *rad* to *warm*, *amped* to *honored*, and I don't mention the enchilada.

Peter says, "I gotta tell you, ever since I heard about that blue-ocean buy you juiced up on Steellyov, I've wanted to step into your AOE. You are one knowledge-dense roxxor."

Uh... blue-ocean quack what?

I don't know what to do with any part of that, so I settle on overt window licking. While I speak of the finesse shown in the Steellyov deal, Volikov's face softens and his brows lift to acknowledge that yes, indeed, he is a rather *accomplished negotiator*.

35

The man is so obviously weakened by this fawning tribute, Peter continues, "What I wouldn't give to have been capital in your team. That must have been the gank of the century."

Volikov nods to agree that, yes, it had been a *particularly ruthless takeover.*

Peter's every word may not be ideal, but his schmoozey performance is internationally appealing. Volikov is relaxed. The assembled Bratva are relaxing. Everything is fixed, and our future is moving along splendidly.

Peter says, "No dissing your gosu skills, but we're here to impress. We've set our growth hackers to peak bandwidth. You and I, we're gonna dominate."

And then, while I'm turning *gosu* into *very impressive* and wondering what to do with the rest, Peter's apple-pie smile returns and he concludes by clapping Volikov on the shoulder and calling him "My comrade."

Cultural mistake #4: Don't—*for fuck's sake*—call a Russian your comrade.

I translate, "My companion."

Volikov's whole demeanor hardens, and he informs me flatly, "He said comrade."

I sound skeptical, "I believe it was companion." But my contradiction works only to further annoy him.

Around us the men are assuring each other, "The *khueplet* said comrade." Questioning, "What the fuck does he mean?" And the driver takes the opportunity to reaffirm, "I told you he was a *pizda s ušami.*"

I lie with greater earnest. "I am certain he said companion." And then, with heavy meaning to Peter: "You definitely said companion because you would *never* say comrade."

"*Never.*" Peter frowns while shaking his head to deny the possibility. Clutching Volikov's hand once more, he leans in to emphasize, "My companion. My homie. *Que pasa, mi amigo?*" And the smile that convinces everyone he's stupid returns.

I'd rather eat my lips than contribute any further to our demise.

And Volikov, in a bid not to reveal his thoughts, also rolls his lips between his teeth, but the squint in his eye betrays the look of calculated acceptance. He's agreed to be amused. He tightens his hold on Peter's hand, cocks his head, and surprises me by replying, "Byla ne byla, priyatel." There was, there wasn't, pal. Or, as the spirit of it has it, Whatever, dude.

And even though Peter has no idea what Volikov said, they laugh together.

But they laugh alone.

The polar bear grumbles, the driver spits on the sidewalk, and the gentleman in the smoking jacket shouts orders that sees Louis Vuitton and Elvis throwing our luggage into the back of the Unimog. Before James Dean gets any closer with the idea of separating me from my travel bag of pharmaceuticals, I catch up with Volikov and Peter who have clamped onto each other's shoulders and, like old friends reunited, are making for the Jaguar.

They seem to have no further use for me.

One is saying jocularly, "We will drive out to Velsk to meet Konstantin. You will like the scenery."

37

While the other is extending the invitation, "Come with us to the Ritz. We'll have the porter throw our luggage in the room while we get breakfast."

One asks, "Da?"

So the other quips, "Da da da dum!"

And because it's all so darn amusing, neither cares if it makes any sense.

The Chariot

Maybe you've seen the video of two naked men on bicycles jousting with flaming spears, or the five men laughing uncontrollably as a brown bear begins an attack that will kill three of them. There's also the one where a man chases and kills a wild boar with a porcelain sink, and another where a military jet buzzes the highway at twenty feet.

A fair question to ask is "Drunk or Russian?"

The correct answer is "Da." Yes.

Russian men haven't gained their stereotype falsely either. Mix boredom and alcohol with a deadly sense of humor and you get Russian Roulette. Russians are known for playing a lethal game of chance with just about everything that can kill a person (i.e., flaming spears, wild animals, and Mach2 power).

And they outdrink the rest of the world by three to one.

The classic caricature of a Russian knocking back shot after shot of vodka is not a misrepresentation.

Volikov is a gray-suited business man—educated, sophisticated, and so successful he has nothing to prove—but he's a silovik who is not going to be bested by the Bratva. At the moment, he's one against three. The driver, the front seat passenger, and the Armani-slippered Felix, who sits at Volikov's side, are Zomanov's men.

Peter and I aren't really expected to compete, but we're here nonetheless.

In the back of the Jaguar, the double bench seats allow Peter and Volikov to keep up a steady stream of face-to-face banter that neither particularly desires to understand.

Peter jokes, "Federal sentencing laws are what determine corporate values," while Volikov blithely talks over him, "Of course communism was an easy victory, but when capitalism overthrew democracy…"

And neither looks to me or pauses for translation.

I could spend the time watching the farms zip past, but the dark tinted windows do little to enhance the scenery, so instead, I try to decipher a tea leaf-styled fortune from the burnt holes in Felix's smoking jacket. The fingers of his left hand rest in his lap and are tattooed with an ace of clubs, a sword, a solid band, and a skull. Tobacco ash has seared a concentrated pattern nearest the club, which suggests the trouble in his future will not be of his own making.

After every shot of vodka, Felix rolls and lights another cigarette. He's got a tremor that looks like Parkinson's, so it takes the same amount of time for him to roll the cigarette as it does for him to light it and then shake the embers across his lap. He adds to the trouble but gains little from it.

After more than a dozen cigarettes, the car is a haze of white smoke and each passenger has inhaled nearly as much nicotine as Felix, but that's hardly the only shared intoxicant. Between each failed attempt to feed his addiction, Felix splashes vodka across the empty glasses until they're full again and then makes a new and innocuous toast. "To our parents" being the most recent.

The introductory "To our meeting" was when Peter and I first entered the car.

Russian tradition dictates that every man (not woman) present drink until the bottles are empty and the last person satiated, and the only acceptable refusal is to pass entirely out. So it is that two hours and twelve shots of vodka later, it's 7:00 a.m. and Peter is dutifully trashed.

During a momentary lull in what passes for conversation, Peter pulls his attention away from Volikov to look out the window. Silver birch trees grow like weeds along the highway's shoulder, and through their spindly branches green fields can be seen. For the first time, it occurs to Peter that we may not be checking into the Ritz Carlton Hotel.

"Slibyl, phlere're we going?"

"Velsk," I explain. "It will be just another seven hours."

"Fluck me."

"You're doing good."

"The fluuck I am."

There's a break in the timely distribution of drinks as Felix stops to smother a particularly hot cinder on his thigh, so Volikov takes the bottle to pour four more shots. I stopped at three; the driver was stopped at nine. There are three empty bottles in the floor-well and one close to empty in Volikov's hand. A full bottle rests beside Felix, but he's also covered in as much, so I'm afraid at any moment he'll go up in flames. Acting as a coffee table is one unopened case, and there's an estimated twenty more in the back of the Land Rover.

Peter has every right to be worried, and that's without him knowing about the plan to double the stock in Velsk. It seems we're driving out to Konstantin's country dacha in Bereznik, and no one trusts the vodka there not to either blind a man or kill him.

Felix explains, "The village good stuff is half vodka, half lighter fluid."

There doesn't seem much point in concerning Peter with that detail either.

The sooner he passes out, the sooner the three remaining Russians can get serious and dick whip each other

41

into submission. Because, really, that's what this manly display is about.

Peter doesn't believe it, but he genuinely is doing well. For an American. Before sinking into oblivion, he manages to throw back eight more shots, which is twenty in total, or three shots over a fifth.

It's 9:30 a.m.

*   *   *

At noon, there are eight empty bottles in the floor-well and the first Russian is down. When he wakes, he'll argue it wasn't his fault because he clonked his head on the window when the driver swerved to miss an oncoming truck while passing three cars and two tractor trailers.

This leaves Volikov and Felix, and it seems to me they've been here before. Experience has given them a leery respect for each other, so the pace slows from the recent four shots an hour to two.

Not keen on the company of the other, they turn their unsteady attention to me.

"Morris," Volikov says the name. A full minute passes before he draws a deep enough breath to complete his thought. "What does he really think he is going to get from this?"

I do as I've been instructed and deny any knowledge. "I'm afraid I cannot say. M and H executives do not share their plans outside the boardroom, so I honestly do not know."

"Feh." Volikov is dismissive. "American men tell everything to their wives."

Also their girlfriends, mistresses, and bartenders, but as I've been told to lie about that, I stick with pedantic details, "Perhaps, but I am not yet Peter's wife."

The same wild swerve that knocked the passenger unconscious also splayed my future husband across the back seat. I hold his head in my lap. Every few minutes I realize I am yet again running my fingers through his hair, and I force myself to stop. It looks like I'm mommy-coddling him, and that's not a good look.

Volikov inspects his hands and says absently, "I suppose after they fill the big Swedish contract, Morris and Hugo will cash out and withdraw."

I almost shake my head to deny it.

"I would prefer to work with merchant traders in Russia, but Morris has made promises too big to ignore." He leans forward to ask with conspiratorial secrecy, "Do you think Hugo knows?"

"Well, of course."

Sinking back in his seat, he drops his chin to his chest and sighs alcoholic vapors. "They say they are selling us short to gain control of the market, but we know it is a resource dump."

I can't let him think that, so I say, "Not at all. They have structured for twenty years."

"Unlikely. It is not like they have found more buyers."

But they have.

Volikov reads my expression and responds, "None as dependable as the Swedes."

My eyes narrow to question him and I practically laugh.

Volikov studies me before waving it away. "Never mind the deal with my fellow Russians—"

And I nod my head to agree.

"—it is the other one I do not trust."

"The Fins?"

"*Noooo...* the *other* one."

Well, that only leaves, "The Germans."

"*The Germans!* Yes, they are the ones. What is the name of that company again?"

"I forget."

"It starts with...? What was it? *Mmmm?* No. *Brraa?* No, that is not it. *Sssscrrree? GghhhrraaaaAA? Aaaaai—?*"

Before his eyebrows fuse with his hairline, I mutter, "Aijan."

"*Aijan!* Yes, thank you. I have a terrible time remembering the name."

I start to wonder if Volikov is playing me for—

"Paper!" he exclaims.

And I'm startled out of my mind.

"Toilet paper, printer paper, newspaper, do you know Russia imports most of its paper needs?"

"I was recently told this."

"We sell our resources raw and then import them again as finished product. We lose billions a year."

"It is unfortunate."

"Morris thinks so too. He says he can change it."

"Oh?"

"He has a grand design to update the Soviet infrastructure." Volikov's expression goes from amused to skeptical. "But I have never heard of a merchant trader investing for long-term advantage."

I try to clarify. "M and H are less merchant traders than facilitators. They adapt to the situation."

"But they will never refurbish the sawmill." Volikov sounds depressed.

I repeat what he already knows. "There is no other option. Federal export tax on round wood ensures no timber leaves Russia unmilled. It has to be cut to be profitable."

"Yes, this is correct." He appears momentarily cheered, but then pessimism hits him hard, and he says gloomily, "But they will never reopen the paper mill."

I want him to be happy again, so I argue, "Why would they not? The pulpwood is free, the paper will pay for itself, and there is absolutely no competition."

"This is true. The paper mill will profit largely, but access to the timber is limited by the lack of roads. Morris and Hugo will never pay to extend the roads."

No, they won't, and they should never have made the promise. But worse than the lie is their smug amusement the deception was believed. Ashamed for us all, I look away.

"No," Volikov repeats with more certainty, "they will never pay for the roads."

The view outside hasn't changed in hours, and by the way I'm staring into the young taiga forest, it may seem I have an unending fascination for trees, but I hardly notice as I'm instead mentally berating myself for being such an easy target.

It's not entirely my fault: I'm a Gemini. I'm chatty, I'm amenable, and I can't shut the hell up.

45

And Volikov is a Scorpio. They have a reputation for being devious manipulators and straight-faced liars. Combine that with their almost innate ability to perceive a person's thoughts from the smallest physical movements and you get the most feared and maligned sign in the zodiac.

As if it wasn't bad enough in the heavens alone, Volikov was also an officer in the FSB.

There are scores of people who have never recovered, or *been* recovered, from an FSB interrogation.

They're a hard organization to describe because nothing like the FSB exists in the USA. To get even remotely close, you'd have to ask the CIA to birth a seven-headed hydra with the faces of the FBI, DEA, NSA, Immigration, Border Patrol, Coast Guard, and the Navy Seals with a hangover and a grudge.

Once known as the KGB, the FSK became the FSB and—damn all notion of oversight—they answer only to the president.

Even if Volikov wasn't a Scorpio with double 6 and 9 on his astral chart, he'd still be dangerous. And I don't really like being in the car with him.

I don't care to be the focus of his attention. He's a snake with double V fangs on either side of his name.

Before he draws from me every secret I know, I turn to Felix as a possible escape. On the back of his hand is a prominent tattoo, so I seize the opportunity to ask, "What does the scarab symbolize?"

"A pickpocket." Then looking down to his trembling hand, Felix acknowledges, "But not anymore."

Volikov asks, "How do Hugo and Morris expect to succeed if they do not extend the roads?"

46

I'd rather slap on a gypsy turban and give a full psychic reading than talk about timber with Volikov again, so I ignore him and say to Felix, "In Egyptian mythology, the scarab symbolizes not only creation but rebirth. You might consider it a second life."

"What about a third?"

"It can be as many as the sun sets and rises."

Volikov is sardonic. "Perhaps he will be immortal."

Felix looks hopeful, so I explain, "Humans only achieve immortality through legend, and legends tend to die poorly."

Volikov seems to choke, and when I look, he's staring at me like I'm more than just foreign.

He finally pulls above his disgust to say, "The birth of a legend is the death of a hero. Every man wishes to die a hero. A hero's death is glorious!"

Despite that much of English literature exists solely to support this idea, I have never heard it so plainly spoken or so fervently believed.

I think perhaps all men must feel this way because Felix seems positively zealous in his corroboration. "A hero's death is glorious!" He can't sling the vodka at the glasses fast enough to make the first exclamation stand for a toast, so he shouts it again, "A hero's death is glorious!"

And I'm too alarmed not to drink as well. But it's a mistake.

Volikov doesn't drink. He's far too angry to drink. He's so furious he's developed a twitch that also looks like Parkinson's, and he's just one neural misfire away from backhanding someone.

The likely recipient will be Felix, who is laughing. Bent at the waist, he's positively hysterical, and it quickly becomes clear that he holds no such view but is instead mocking Volikov—derisively, hilariously, spit-in-your-face, mocking the silovik.

It's 1:00 p.m.

*   *   *

Today's literature was yesterday's popular trash and Russian history doesn't do a lot to support the State hero among the underclass. The hero of Volikov's imagination barely exists in nineteenth- or twentieth-century Russian literature. The women are heroic, but the men are largely villains, cowards, or so intellectually tortured they end the tale in an asylum.

Russian Romanticism, Sentimentalism, and Realism were almost harder on the male hero than satire.

Parody was the first weapon of the poor, but the Bolsheviks largely did away with that as well.

But true contempt for authority wasn't really born until Stalin's gulags.

And while Felix is just a couple of decades too young to have known the worst, he is still a direct product of the hate fostered in those camps.

To die a national hero is likely the worst fate Felix can imagine. Serving the State would make him a living receptacle into which greater men pleasure themselves to climax, which in prison parlance is a goat, and as Felix tells Volikov, "Yob tvoyu kosyols." Fuck your goats.

Peter begins to stir upright and mumbles in response, "Yobs to you too, cozy yocals."

48

Lest he unwittingly says something intelligible in either language, I push his head back into my lap.

Volikov responds to Felix, "You fucked enough goats for us both."

Which kind of sounds like, "Who does not know, huh, boy?" so I close Peter's mouth.

Felix replies, "Ya yebal tvoju mat."

And Peter repeats, "I fucked your mother."

Like some kind of wild animal that might be calmed by throwing a sack over its head, I cover Peter's with my hastily removed cardigan.

Felix is quick to assume. "The *huesos* speaks Russian."

And I'm way too quick to deny. "No, the cocksucker doesn't."

Volikov calls Felix "Muda´k." Asshole.

And Peter bolts upright. "*Muzak?* I hate Muzak. Whoa…" He sucks at the black fabric that covers his face. "Thiz iz the darkest elevator… Sibyl, I can't see shit. What floor iz thiz?"

I pull the sweater from his head and, "Oh," he sees, "floor über Russki."

"Yeah," I agree, "it's über Russki in here."

Besides the two angry Russians, there's a fog of alcohol in the air that's turned the cigarette smoke into a psychoactive inhalant. Peter could pitch this to Marlboro as an intoxicating aerosol.

He says to Volikov, "I think we can safely remove the hose from the exhaust now."

But Volikov is ten shots drunker than when Peter last saw him, and during the interval, he lost his sense of humor.

49

He's not amused, but he's decided to keep Peter close. He says, "I would be interested to hear how many kilometers of roads Morris and Hugo have budgeted for." And this time he wants it translated. He looks to me and then throws his chin toward Peter as if to say, *Tell him.*

I don't really want to, but I do.

Disconcertingly quick to reach sobriety, Peter's smile is warm for Volikov, but his question is chilled for me. "Baby, what have you two been talking about?"

"A bit of this and that."

"A bit of which and what exactly?"

"Oh, you know: tattoos, heroes, goats, trees."

"Trees?"

I point out the window. "It's been hours of trees."

"That *is* what I'm afraid of."

"I know, right? Bears. The woods are full of them."

"I'm not afraid of bears, Sibyl."

"You should be. Have you seen the size of them?"

"What did you—"

"They're not black bears like at home, but brown. Big difference."

"—tell them about—"

"They don't bluff like black bears."

"—the trees?"

"Did you know the brown bear has only recently been accepted in Russia as a national symbol?"

"You literally make my brain hurt."

I reach into the bag at my feet to offer, "Aspirin?"

*　*　*

The way to tell if a corporate citizen like Peter is particularly serious is if they start using words in a manner Merriam-Webster would approve. In fury, retribution, and admonishment, executives want no misunderstanding, and they can become explicitly, and unexpectedly, articulate.

If it weren't for anger, I'd have little idea Peter was capable of conversing in commonly recognizable phrases.

For the very fear he's about to become too plainly spoken, I want to fill his mouth with something less dangerous. I separate an authentic aspirin from the Bayer bottle and then look to Felix for another toast to help Peter swallow what I hand him.

Volikov stares at the exchange, so I offer up the bottle. "Aspirin?"

"*Feh.*" He's again dismissive.

I falsely argue its benefits, "You will not get a headache if you take one now."

To Felix, I fabricate further, "And recovery time is halved."

Looking at Peter, I sound genuinely apologetic, "It is almost an unfair advantage."

Volikov snorts, "I will try your aspirin."

I don't wait for Felix to assent; I just go ahead and give him a sleeping pill as well.

His toast is portentous. "To women."

Determined to put Peter back in my lap, the shots increase from two an hour to the original six again, but only Peter makes it past three.

51

Felix tries to shake off the effect of the zopiclone, but the head snap meant to deliver mental clarity only manages to throw him against Volikov's shoulder.

"Steady there, hoss." Peter reaches out to lend a hand but withdraws when he hears Volikov's lip blubbering snore. "Nah, he won't mind."

The driver looks in the rearview mirror and says with disgust, "Duraki." Fools. He looks at the front seat passenger, who hasn't so much moved in the last hours as slipped so deep into sleep his head has left a streak of hair gel down the window to the armrest, and says again, "Durák."

Peter announces brightly, "I'm feeling pretty buffed for this level."

And I smile to hear his return to linguistic obscurity.

The Fool

Velsk is ramshackle and rundown, and I suspect only a winter setting and a very foreign eye might see it as quaint. Six months ago it would have been covered in snow and obscured by dark, but now it's midsummer so the sun is still high at 5:00 p.m. Nothing goes unobserved. Not the rot, or the weeds, or the drunks accompanied by stray horses in the street.

If the horses weren't grazing from potholes, they might be induced by traffic to seek the security of the sidewalk, but innumerable birch saplings have ripped through the footpaths, so the road remains a safer location for both man and beast.

It's hard to know exactly where the countryside gave way to this overgrown town, but it's very evident that residents of neither care about landscaping.

A hundred years ago, the timber houses that crowd the street might have been tidy, but now they've faded into every dull color except pretty and the land grows wild with grass.

While there are hundreds of occupied homes, there is no discernible business district, and I can't imagine where the men intend to procure twenty more cases of vodka.

Our phones show Russia's tourism site promoting "2 things to do in Velsk!" Both are hotels. One is a gray Communist block and the other still appears to be a barn.

The town is wretchedly poor and terribly neglected, yet it's infinitely preferable to any trailer park.

I have lived in worse, and Peter has evidently never seen anything close.

His most charitable estimation is to note, "Nothing a day of carpet bombing wouldn't improve."

He thumbs between the two tourist attractions and asks, "Which will it be? A night with Stalin or baby Jesus?"

But we're not going to either hotel. The convoy of cars slows to a halt to turn into a tight gravel drive. Unlike the other houses that cramp the street, beyond the mailbox is an acre of long weeds and a two-story turquoise mansion, of sorts. Like most of the nineteenth-century dwellings we've passed, the same wide and intricate folk carvings decorate the windows, doors, and roof, but here the scale is massive. Made of clapboard, it's heavily weathered and the wood is more stained a shade of seasick blue than painted.

It's crooked and swayed and collapsing, and it looks distinctly like a firetrap, but I'd sell everything Peter owns to possess it.

I'm enthralled with it.

Peter, on the other hand, is differently moved. He whispers, "I am actually afraid."

"Of what?"

He looks from me back to the hulking mass of decay and whimpers a laugh that implies he's mystified by my lack of understanding.

Because weeds are brushing the sides of the car as we park, I'm not entirely certain, but I think he murmurs, "I have no idea where I am."

But Peter's horror can't match that of the Bratva who open the doors on the Jaguar expecting to haul forth two unconscious Americans but find instead Felix and Volikov inextricably passed out in each other's arms.

The driver stalks away from the scene cursing, "Kucha durakov," Bunch of fools, and the front seat passenger gets the door yanked from under his head so he's left half dangling from the car.

Someone whistles under their breath, "Eto polniy pizdetz." This is a full fuckup.

And Peter, because he is not—or possibly because he is—incredibly stupid, takes the opportunity to pour a parting shot of vodka. Lifting the glass to his mouth, he downs it quickly and mechanically, as though he were utterly bored with this too often repeated ritual. Then, gently and without hurry, he straightens the cuffs of his shirt and steps from the car an American god.

* * *

Peter has masterfully played the moment, and for the moment, it's hard to know whether the Bratva or I have for him more admiration.

Whatever fear he had for the derelict mansion, he shows none of it now. In fact, he shows little of anything because he's remembered not to smile.

He's never been more attractive.

A woman at the mansion's open door raises one brow in appreciation, and another on the steps wets her lips in interest. And while they are both strikingly beautiful, considering all the tattooed men in the yard wearing wife-beaters, I figure they're both too detrimentally stupid to be a threat.

Of greater concern are all the tattooed men in the yard wearing wife-beaters.

A quick count of twelve tells me I don't have enough sleeping pills to get Peter safely through the weekend.

55

There are going to be more cases of vodka than I have zopiclone. And I'm not about to give any of these criminals Ambien because even normal drunks on Ambien become entirely too unpredictably weird. And hell, already, there's a man with a polar bear on his head.

He's just one of the fifteen oddities. James Dean, Elvis, and the blond with cornrows now seem relatively ordinary when compared to the circus-styled strongman, fat man, and too many tattooed men to be considered freaks.

Peter points for me to stand at his side and instructs, "Stop gawking."

I really should, but it's difficult when they're all staring back.

And because they're Russian, not one of them is smiling, so the welcoming party—if that's what it is—doesn't come across as particularly hospitable.

It occurs to me that maybe I don't know where I am either.

It also strikes me that Volikov and Felix are the ones who give and maintain order, and as they're in no condition to take charge, the group is without direction.

Their opinion of the two Americans is still unformed. Are we to be accepted or derided?

It's a delicate time while they try to make up their minds.

They're not speaking, or even really moving, and yet, in their languid interest, I feel aggression.

I'd like to take Peter's hand, but he's playing it cool, wading into their midst, showing no concern whatsoever.

From his Fifth Avenue-styled hair to his Italian leather shoes, the Bratva are sizing him up, and he's lazily returning their attention, looking each man in the eye.

As he makes his slow way through the curious ensemble to the woman at the front door, he's stopped by an ink-covered hand thrown across his chest. When he looks with warning down the length of the tattooed arm to the face, the hand flips to offer a cigarette.

Peter accepts and then leans into the flame offered by another heavily inked arm.

The flame bearer says, "International flight and a nine-hour drive, and you are still hard as my *konfetku*." Konfetku = candy = dick, and I'm not translating that to Peter for their amusement.

And I don't need to because the accusatory tone has already riled him, so after a confrontational round of alpha male glaring, Peter blows smoke toward the house and asks, "Konstantin?"

The man who offered the cigarette raises his brows while turning his mouth into an exaggerated frown and suggests, "You would be very brave to interrupt him now," and a chuckle runs through the yard.

Because this exchange seems likely to devolve into some sort of chest-beating shit-slinging territorial display of masculinity, I translate verbatim.

Peter responds, "Nice house. Is it yours?"

"Nyet."

"Konstantin's?"

The circus finds this hilariously contemptible.

The Fat Man explains, "House belongs to translator."

57

Peter says, "I'd like to meet him."

Half the men fold with laughter, and the rest shake their heads in dismay.

Peter holds his ground, staring at the strongman until the strongman says, "Translator will say *hello* when he wants to speak fat American language."

For most Russians, the English language seems unnecessarily full of padding. All those *his* and *hers* and *a*'s and *the*'s, it's plump with needless words. I might explain this to Peter but it's not really the sort of thing that interests him, and whoever is pulling in the drive does.

He stares at the modest black Volga rolling through the weeds until it stops beside the Unimog.

The strongman throws his chin toward the new arrival and says, "My favorite *gondon*."

Gondon = condom = sorry excuse for a man.

True to the picture provided by M&H's Competitive Intelligence Department, Isaak Madulin steps from the car a cloud of gray. Gray hair, gray pallor, gray suit, and pulling an even grayer expression, I don't think he wants to be here.

With his long gangly legs, he could stride from his car to the tension of the big tent in four easy steps, but instead, each forward footfall is small and overly managed and seems in favor of retreat.

Peter tries to help. Extending his hand, he stalks the short distance, saying, "Mr. Madulin, I can't tell you how eager I am to sit down with you and have a conversation for possibility."

Looking dully over the rabble, Isaak cuts short my translation to say, "Before they start chewing on our bones, we should talk in the house."

The Hermit

Russians don't decorate like Americans. To start, there is a complete deficit of plush furnishings. Every chair is straight backed hard, and the couch will be designed on nineteenth-century aesthetics, suitable only for women in corsets so tight they're incapable of considering anything worse. The rooms are often large, but all the furniture will be pushed against opposite walls so there exists in the center a vast area of empty space. Coffee table? Don't be absurd. But there will always be some sort of monstrous cabinet looming in a corner with at least six drawers and a dozen locked doors. And you will never see anyone use it ever.

In the winter, the rooms are eighty degrees, but in the summer, you'll be lucky if the high reaches sixty.

In the mansion's front parlor, I'm cold and uncomfortable. Ten feet to my left, I hear the creak of wood as Peter adjusts for comfort in the antique Empire chair, and fifteen feet in front of us, across a wide expanse of elaborate parquet, six-foot Isaak sits in the center of a dainty matching couch, knees nearly level with his chest.

The only one who looks happy is the cat on top of the cupboard. From far across the room, I can see the single overhead light reflecting orange in the dark circles of his eyes.

In contrast, Isaak's pupils are pinpoints of black lost in two globes of ocean blue euphoria. Opiate addiction. I don't need it explained because I already saw it in his astral chart.

He's a Pisces with a Chinese Tiger in the water, and he's also ruled by the number seven.

Perhaps it would be fair to warn I'm about to devolve into some serious occult nonsense here, so if you can't bear the esoteric prattle, feel free to skip down a couple paragraphs.

For those that remain, let's have a quick lesson in numerology.

This is way oversimplified, but the basic goal of numerology is to render from words, dates, and symbols a single meaningful number. In the case of birth, this number is achieved by adding the month, day, and year. Isaak Madulin was born March 13, 1962, which is also 03-13-1962, so we add 0+3+1+3+1+9+6+2 and then take the total of 25 and add 2+5 for 7.

In the alphabet, A, B, C, D is 1, 2, 3, 4 and so on, until the letter I reaches 9 and then circles back to J to become 1 again.

Trust me, Isaak Madulin is a seven.

With both his name and date of birth equaling seven, Isaak couldn't be more of a seven.

And seven, because of its offset location on the Tree of Life, is the lowest degradation of the soul. Things shouldn't get any worse than seven.

But making things worse, Isaak's particular 1962 model of Tiger is ruled by Water, as is the astrological sign Pisces.

In the Tarot, water is represented by the Cups, and the Seven of Cups is the fetid cascading fountain called Debauch.

I wouldn't be the first to call the Seven of Cups the most dismal card in the deck, and this is Isaak's card. Unlike most people, whose name will equal one number and their date of birth another, whose Western astrological element might be Water and their Chinese may be Earth, where these variations would supply four different Tarot cards with a chance for multiple and unique interpretations in the story they told, Isaak has just one: the Seven of Cups. Debauch.

Humor me while I wrap up my hair in a silk turban and explain the Seven of Cups: *It is a chalice of poison that promises ecstasy but delivers regret. To consume what it offers is to pursue false desires and sink into artificial security. It is pleasure corrupted. It is somnolent addiction in every form, but especially opium. Swilling from this cup will lead to acts of depravity so obscene the conscious mind will reel away in shame, but still the drinker will not stop as the easiest way to soothe the humiliation is to drink again. In this cycle of vice and despair, the only chance of escape may seem suicide, but this is often just the final and ultimate submission to the cup, as death will likely result from overdose.*

Just to be clear, there is absolutely nothing good to be found in the Seven of Cups.

Now, I don't honestly and definitively believe anything I just said about numerology and the Tarot, and yet I need no further proof that Isaak is a thoroughly degenerate opiate addict.

Blame my dual nature as a Gemini: I believe none of it and all of it. Simultaneously. The only sign that has it worse is Libra. Now they're really hopeless when it comes to picking a side because they see all sides equally. But as we presently don't have any Libras to deal with, never mind them.

For now, we have the Seven of Cups and the Prince of Coins, and the conversation is stressed because few cards are more at odds.

One seeks nearly suicidal pleasure through the psychoactive alterations of his senses, and the other gets his kicks from the acquisition of property.

One is already bored. "Everything worth doing happened two decades ago."

While the other is still trying to get business started. "It's that kind of forward thinking, with its roots firmly planted in the past, which will allow us to grow to a high altitude view."

Isaak stares at me as though I were the mother of that abomination. He allows a few moments of silence to bury my translation firmly in the past and then continues, "The big game was played in the nineties."

And Peter has me return, "We're here to take it to the next level."

The cold contempt in Isaak's eyes crosses the sea of parquet and creates a chill down my spine. He tries again. "The problem with post-Soviet reforms was gangsters were doing business with the *nomenklatura*, and neither knew the rules by which the other played."

And Peter would have me respond, "Sounds like a real circular firing squad."

But I'm not inclined to repeatedly test the temperament of an opiate addict, so instead I ask, "Who made you director of the saw mill? The Bratva or the siloviki?"

"*M-dá.*" *Pff*. "Maksim Volikov made that happen. He makes everything happen in my life: director of sawmill, mayor of Bereznik, Chief Operating Officer of Konstantin Imperiya. My wife takes too much pleasure in calling me a *krémljad*."

Krémljad: a conjunction of Kremlin and bljad (whore).

"Baby"—Peter smiles to appear relaxed—"I can't say anything to make this man happy, and now he's sneering. Why is he sneering?"

I explain, "Volikov installed Isaak as the director of the saw mill, mayor of Bereznik, and COO of KI. Now his wife thinks he's a silovik vassal."

Peter blinks. He stops breathing, stops smiling, and then blinks twice more. He's ten feet away, but I think he mumbles, "The fuck we get here?"

Isaak pulls Peter's attention back by speaking again. "I was a twenty-four-year-old law graduate with plans to rise through the ranks of the Young Reformers in Moscow, but Maksim tells me—" Isaak looks to me and instructs, "You tell Peter what I say."

So I do.

"Maksim says to me, 'Go to Bereznik and take care of sawmill for me. When this is done, there will be a position waiting for you in Moscow.'"

He pauses for me to tell Peter.

"I do for Maksim everything he asks. I take over directorship of the sawmill. I alter the books to show the factory is running at a loss. I bribe government auditors to confirm it is in deficit. And I put it forward to the government that this factory needs to be privatized immediately or it will drain the dwindling resources of the State."

Peter nods to show he understands everything I told him.

"None of this was easy because this sawmill was very productive and everyone wanted a bribe."

Peter nods again.

"I arrange for the sawmill to be sold at auction, but it is meant to be a paper auction. You understand?"

He doesn't, but he agrees nonetheless.

63

"No one is going to bid because everyone knows Maksim Volikov of the KGB—*errr...*" Isaak growls and frowns to correct himself. "Not KGB but FSB." Then he waves away the notion it is anything but, and explains, "KGB, FSB, it is the same."

"Right," Peter confirms.

"So no one is going to bid because Maksim Volikov of the KGB has approval from the Federal Forestry Agency to buy the Bereznik sawmill."

Peter says, *"Mmm hmm."*

"Then he learns Konstantin has offered double his bribes and has already paid to buy all the leases for the land. It is called a lease, but in reality, Konstantin owns the whole of the Bereznik forest."

Peter cocks his head, lifts his brows, and half smirks in appreciation.

"Yes, he is a very shrewd man. Normally, a man such as Maksim and one such as Konstantin would kill each other over something like the sawmill. Because both knew this, both went into hiding."

Peter can't quite get the smile off his face.

"Many meetings took place between myself, as a representative for Maksim, and Felix, as the advisor to the Zomanov Bratva. In the end, we came to the arrangement you now enter."

Peter stops smiling.

"Konstantin owns the company in name, but Maksim and I own majority control through shares."

Peter listens to me translate but stares at Isaak. Peter is unreadable.

64

And Isaak is quiet for a long time. He runs his hand repeatedly over the worn velvet of the antique couch as though he were lost entirely to an opiate dream. Finally, the silence is interrupted when the cat jumps from the cabinet to the floor and the thump of impact seems to shake the mansion.

Jolted back to the moment, Isaak stops caressing the couch to ask, "So, Peter, whose signature do you imagine is most valuable in closing your deal?"

*   *   *

"Baby, I'm not trying to wrong side you, but we need to align on Isaak's meaning because what you said sounded like some back-of-the-envelope conversion." Peter seems to doubt my fluency in Russian. "Could you have been directionally accurate but off-road?"

I've answered *No* to every variation of the same metaphor for fifteen minutes, so I've resorted to ignoring Peter in preference to staring at our luggage. There's no point in unpacking because in the morning we're off to Konstantin's country dacha in Bereznik, and besides, the second-floor room we've been given contains only a swayback double bed and two eighteenth-century chairs. I've put his bag on one chair and mine on the other.

"I know you mastered a big learn, but even a ten percent delta in error would impact. Were you and Isaak level-set?"

Nothing in this house is level. The floors warp high over the joists, and the doors hang at a five-degree slant.

"My sense check tells me you might have gone tangentery."

Tangentery. Tangential? Of or relating to a tangent? Perhaps a straight line? No, those don't exist here either.

"Not to disenthuse, but you have to cognisize, this is no baked cake."

While Peter worries over my Russian, I feel like I'm losing my grasp of English.

From downstairs, I hear shouted, "Chto iz etogo? Yesli ya umru, ya umru." I doubt they're quoting Lermontov, but, in *A Hero of Our Time*, Pechorin asks the same question, "What of it? If I die, I die." Russian I've got.

English, though...

"If you're more than a nine iron off, we're looking at a two comma punt."

No hero of any work has ever uttered that phrase.

Peter pleads, "Baby, just give me a binary answer."

So I respond, "One."

"One?"

"Perhaps you'd prefer zero."

"No, Sibyl. Binary means yes or no. Just *yes* or *no*."

"No, then."

"Huh?"

"No, I did not provide a back-of-the-envelope translation. No, I did not go off-road, tangentery, or punt the nine iron through a two comma goal post. Isaak definitely implied the signature you require to close the deal is not Konstantin's but one of the silovik." *Okhuye ́t'. Fucking hell.*

The Star

The driver with the bull tattoo is still seeing red. He stands in the front parlor with his back to the huge cupboard and glares with suspicion and hatred at Peter.

He, Peter, and the eleven other Bratva in the room are ten shots into the seventh bottle to be opened since we came downstairs, and because Peter arrived sober, he was also obligated to down a full drinking glass of vodka, so add another five shots to his ten.

Twenty-two ounces of 88 proof is guaranteed to have just about anyone annihilated within an hour, so it's not surprising Peter is leaning from his chair at a steeper angle than the doors.

And because the night is always just beginning in the Russian summer, this group has not even started to get staggered. Peter is too far gone to be afraid anymore, but I am worried for him.

James Dean asks, "Why are we inside while the sun still shines?"

And the Polar Bear answers, "We finish this case, then we shoot boar."

I'm hoping the subsequent fifteen shots of which the Polar Bear speaks will put Peter safely on his face before this crowd arms with rifles. Then again, they're Russian, so they might just as easily be hunting with derringers or cannons. It matters little which as Peter has fired none.

To the Fat Man and Elvis, Peter is wagging his finger. "I see your look of anticipointment, but I assure you, my bouncebackability is in recoil." Gesturing to the empty glasses, he insists, "Rebound shots for a win."

While opening the eighth bottle, Louis Vuitton happens to note, "The *mudozvon* is about to fall from his chair."

Mudozvon: a man making music with his balls.

One of the tattooed men hands Peter a hunk of bread with the suggestion, "Hold this in your front teeth. When you kiss the floor, you will not break your smile."

To which Peter exclaims, "Pumpernickel rye? I'll pump her quarters dry!"

I roll my eyes. *What an anecgloat.*

As they continue in this uninterpreted conversation, the Bull wants me to explain, "Why are you with him?"

"To translate."

His nostrils flare with annoyance before he clarifies, "How much money does he have?"

The Polar Bear's white muzzle swings in my direction and also waits for an answer.

To blatantly ask about your finances is such a Russian norm, I should not be insulted. If Peter manages to remain conscious, he won't see dusk without someone asking him the same question. Only they won't be calling him a gold digger.

Peter has never had to dig. He's the Prince of Coins; gold is his birthright. And the Bratva, tattooed from their crowns to their toes, are so perfectly versed in symbolism they can see it.

And they can apparently see me for what I am as well. There is to this revelation no small amount of shame. It burns red into my cheeks.

The Bull is roused. He says, "This is a man's night. You do not belong here. Come, I will show you something."

68

While I turn my head to refuse, the Polar Bear asks, "You see other women?" The ears shake back and forth in denial. He looks to Peter, affixing a vodka label to his forearm like a tattoo, and assures, "Do not worry. He is safe. Go with Demyan."

*   *   *

I doubt Peter has noticed I've left the parlor to follow the Bull named Demyan into the kitchen, and this negligence has all of a sudden become a worry because the Bull is saying, "I will show you what it is to be a man."

This is chiefly disturbing because Demyan is dropping his pants to the floor.

Looking quickly to the ceiling, I ask, "What in Christ's name?"

And he tries to call my attention back with, "I have two."

"I am sure you do."

"Look."

"I never doubted it, so there is no need to prove it."

"They are larger than most people expect."

"Unquestionably."

"If you do not deserve them, the brotherhood will scrub them off with steel wool."

...millions of voices suddenly cried out in terror...

"Are you going to look?"

"Do you really need me to?"

"Have you seen them before?"

69

"Once or twice."

"Do you know what they mean?"

"I swear to god, no."

"I got them when I was twenty."

"That is rather late."

"No, that is very young." His tone is now irritated. "Do you know anything about *tatuirovki?*"

Tatuirovki? Tattoos? I look down from the ceiling and—thank the heavens—he's displaying two stars on his knees. And they are very large. Inked in black, the points extend beyond his kneecaps so the northern tips nearly pierce the hulls of darkened sailboats, and the southern rays stretch down his shins to flared cobras.

He asks again, "Do you know what they mean?"

It may seem we're back in territory from which I could safely guess, but the eight-pointed star is found in nearly every culture on Earth, and to each it means something different. Still, the collective unconscious has agreed it's a symbol of great power, and as I mention aloud, "I doubt you would be standing in your cotton briefs if it was not something to brag about."

"They are proof I will bow to no authority."

No bull would.

"Konstantin does not have stars on his knees."

Yes, well, cats abscond before they're asked. And speaking of which, "Where is Konstantin?"

Demyan directs my attention back to the ceiling. From the floor above comes the repetitive thump, creak, and groan of old furniture under duress. He explains the unnecessary, "He has a woman."

Somewhat at a loss in this conversation, I half smirk to say, "So, he has a woman but no stars."

"He has stars on his shoulders. Not his knees."

"The shoulders are where we carry the burdens of the world. Are his stars the burden of authority?"

Standing in his underwear, Demyan catches a laugh, almost smiles, and studies my face to see if the innuendo was intentional.

I wince with self-censure, thinking, *Sibyl, you are a suicidal fool to have made that joke.*

His amusement instantly fades, and he nods with understanding. Bending down to gather his pants, he makes himself decent while saying, "You thought me too much of an animal to read Tolstoy. He was the master of double meaning. But you should not speak like that again."

Regret, I need to start expressing serious regret. I've only just opened my mouth to begin when he looks up and cuts me off. "No, it was funny. To me. It would not be so funny if I were to explain it to them." He points to the parlor.

"I apologize for both the insinuation and underestimating you. I will do neither again."

"You have already done the second again, but you do not know it yet."

"Then, please, correct me."

"No." He levels calculating eyes on me. "I would rather it play out."

"Splendid. I look forward to acting the fool once more."

"Your little anecdote was correct, though. Konstantin's stars show he was once a thief in law, but he does not respect the laws of the thieves or the State. He is only Bratva. A thief in

71

law would never do business with a silovik. Not to benefit the government, anyway." **Catching a humorless laugh in his throat, he admits,** "His stars *are* the burden of authority."

"From how Isaak described it, I was under the impression Konstantin was not willingly doing business with Volikov."

"With Volikov and the sawmill, no. But his rise to Pakhan was government funded."

He does seems quite determined for me to know something, and better sense would have me backing out of the room to join the thieves in a drunken boar hunt, but as Dostoyevsky says, *It takes something more than intelligence to act intelligently.*

"I imagine a government-controlled Pakhan would be quite useful, but did they have a particular purpose in mind?"

"The old nomenklatura needed a liaison to the underworld. Did Morris and Hugo's *Competitive Intelligence Department,*" **he chokes on the words with amusement,** "discover how Konstantin met them?"

"If they did, Peter did not share it."

"He was running a protection racket on the exclusive hotels in Moscow. Gambling, prostitution, you understand? And the whores had connections. Sometime in the early nineties, the mayor of Moscow got into some trouble with a particularly young one and Konstantin fixed it. Five months later, he was funding the mayor's reelection."

I smile with understanding.

"You can see how the hotels and the mayor would place him in Yeltsin's circle, and from there it was just a drink and a cigarette to the other top officials."

I nod.

"The Ministry of Internal Affairs gave him export contracts. In return, he kept the various Bratva families from taking too much. Too much life, too much money, too much territory. Things were very bloody then."

"I recently read this. It was described as a decade of war between the criminal underworld, the New Russians, and the State."

"New Russians," **Demyan repeats with disdain.** "A New Russian's son cries to his daddy, 'Everyone in my school rides the bus. I look like a little bitch in this Ferrari.' The father says, 'Do not worry, son. I will buy you a bus and you will ride like everyone else.'"

Still laughing, I point out, "There is a pin-striped Bentley in the front yard."

"I know. The distinction between Bratva and New Russian is no longer discernible. Some of us thieves find this a problem."

"And you would like to do something about it."

"I would."

"And you have a particular plan in mind."

"I do."

"And it involves Peter."

He smiles to suggest, "His translator will do."

"No. She will not."

The curt refusal has him shedding clothes again. Before I can finish asking "What in Christ's name is it this time?" **the black T-shirt is over his head and flipped around his fist like he plans to punch glass.**

He's unamused.

I'm slack-jawed staring.

73

He's got a nice chest.

I have enough time to take in the grinning devil and the rose wrapped in barbed wire before he turns his back on me. Now the bull beneath the horns is revealed. Head held high, the legs are steeply angled to control a sliding charge. Inked in the dust beneath the hooves is Turgenev: Возьмите для себя, что вы можете и не исключено другими. Take for yourself what you can and do not be ruled by others.

I quote Turgenev back to him, "It is fun talking to you, rather like walking on the edge of a cliff."

Turning around, he completes it, "At first one is nervous, but then, from somewhere, courage takes over."

In the stillness that follows, I slowly reconsider him. I consider not only him but myself, the creed on his back, and the fiancé shouting inanities from the next room. I think about the disgrace of poverty, the fear of homelessness, and the compromises I've made to wipe both from my future. I wonder if Demyan is the Devil revealed in the Tarot. I feel Death enter the room. Change is imminent. It was all in the cards. It's but a simple surrender to fate to agree.

I've been ruled by the promise of gold, the walls of security, the Prince of Coins incarnate, but the Devil is ruled by pride. We're all ruled by something.

You give up one only to be subjugated by another.

But it does seem preferable to bow to the one that causes the least shame.

Still, there's the dishonor of betrayal to consider.

Take for yourself what you can and do not be ruled by others. It's cold and dangerous near the cliffs. Faced with a plunge to freedom or a retreat to safety, courage bows to survival and I say, "Spokoynoy nochi." Goodnight.

The Magus

Fear that I may need to intercede on Peter's behalf and save his life this night means I'm sleeping light. I've taken only one zopiclone, two methaqualone, and four promethazine. For an addict like me, this wouldn't be enough to dull footsteps in the hall, so there was no chance it could mask an explosion. My eyes snap open. Through the sheer curtains of the second-floor bedroom, gray light casts shadows over the walls. It's dusk. Maybe midnight.

The sonic boom that shifted the house is still rocking the weights in the windows.

Sitting up in bed, I wonder if they're hunting with tannerite (kind of like dynamite). I've seen Louisiana hunters turn six wild pigs into a cloud of pink dust with tannerite, and if you think I'm kidding, just go do a quick YouTube search and see for yourself. And if you still have a taste for high velocity pork splatter after that, you might as well go ahead and look up Russians hunting with RPGs, because that's what we've got going here tonight.

Standing at the window, I look over the back of the house. Just past the cars parked in the high grass of the lawn, a narrow clearing cuts through the acres of trees. On a property overgrown with weeds, this alley of death appears to be tended, though whether it's been trampled or bush-hogged is hard to tell.

At the open edge of the corridor, one Bratva holds an RPG tube, two hold spotlights, nine more hold rifles, and Peter holds a revolver, but what makes this Russian Redneck is all thirteen of them hold a drink. The spotlights illuminate the terrified boars trapped in cages at the halfway mark between maniacs and freedom. Squealing through the woods to the next village, the last one to be released has managed to escape with its life.

I watch Elvis load the empty RPG tube with another rocket and feel sick for the terrified swine.

But I'm just as worried for Peter who barely controls a revolver with a ten-inch barrel. I watch in horror as he absently raises one leg to scratch his ankle with the hammer. He stumbles, catches himself with the barrel against the ground, and then, using the length of the pistol as a cane, he somewhat rights himself again. Grass now hangs from the pistol's sights, which Peter tries to clean by swiping against his leg.

Before he blows his kneecaps off, the Polar Bear snarls, "Kakógo chërta," What the hell, and grabs the gun away.

I wonder if I can live with the memory of watching Peter kill himself. Most of me thinks I should probably just take more pills and sleep through it, hear about it in the morning after the body has been removed and the grass washed clean of blood. That might be preferable to a lifetime of flashbacks and nightmares.

Next, I wonder what it would be like to live with the memory of Peter killing a dozen men. As Elvis drops the RPG tube on Peter's shoulder, I feel fairly certain at least a few of them will die.

Twelve Russians, forty dwindling cases of vodka, and an RPG: What could possibly go wrong?

I think things might be put right when I hear Volikov enter the house. He shouts into the hall, "Stop this noise and get me a drink."

At the same time, Felix rounds the corner of the house and crosses the yard. Despite the tremor that shakes his right hand, he looks quite refreshed. He calls out, "Vodka and firearm."

But not that refreshed.

And the Polar Bear seems to notice. He tucks Peter's confiscated revolver into the back of his pants and waves away the Fat Man's offer of an SKS.

Good polar bear.

But then, through the window to my left, I get my first troubling impression of Konstantin. He shouts across the distance, "Give him the grenade launcher." (Of course there's a grenade launcher. Why wouldn't there be? Standard equipment on a boar hunt.)

At the sound of the authoritative voice, Peter swings around on the house, aiming the RPG at its lopsided boards.

"Chërt voz'mí!" Devil take me! I'm pretty certain the heavy thump from next door is the sound of Konstantin throwing himself prostrate to the floor.

Peter doesn't see him. Instead, he sees me. As a roar of protest erupts in the yard, he stops with the rocket aimed at my face to smile and wave.

There's nothing to do but wave back, and then he's wrenched away, his back to the house, the rocket to the boar.

Also facing the boar is right-handed Felix trying to left-hand control a grenade launcher. His right hand jumps uncontrolled on the forward grip; his left flutters around the trigger.

As the group prepares to down another bottle, Felix shouts the toast, "Poyekhali!" Let's get started!

I have no desire to see any of these people kill each other, and I have even less desire to witness the obliteration of trapped boar for a night's drunken amusement. And I need not

77

be aware of either when I've got a bag full of sedatives so powerful they can wipe out consciousness as easily as tannerite.

*　　*　　*

If I'd not topped up one zopiclone, two methaqualone, and four promethazine with four zopiclone, three methaqualone, and two Ambien, I would understand what it means that Peter is sitting on the edge of the bed, hand to his head, rubbing circles around his temples.

I'd like to turn my back on him and return to sleep, but the house is loud with activity and the drugs can barely compete.

Downstairs, someone is shouting, "Load the cases into the Rover," and someone else is booming, "I will take the *Kukurzer,*" Kukurzer = corn cruiser = Toyota Land Cruiser, and then an argument about who is more capable of driving said corn cruiser nearly drowns out the cry of "Put Volikov in the suitcase and Isaak in the coffin."

Suitcase: Mercedes-Benz 600.

Coffin: Chevrolet Tahoe.

From the yard, I hear car doors opening and trunks slamming shut.

Peter looks down to me and says, "These guys are HAMs." *Hard-ass motherfuckers.*

Gently, I reach out to touch his busted and bloody lip.

He says, "Everyone's drunk, no one's been to sleep, and now I think we're racing."

There's a knock at the door, and a voice says, "Leaving in ten. Konstantin is waiting."

"Actually," I tell Peter, "we're all driving out to a dacha in Bereznik this morning. You're going to meet Konstantin in ten minutes."

"The fuck you say?"

"Yes. Ten minutes: Konstantin."

"I'm drunk *and* hung over."

And I'm drugged and fucked up. But admitting that won't help. And Peter needs help. Through the ripped fabric of his pant leg, I rub his mud-covered knee. "You'll do fine. You're a natural charmer. You can do this in your sleep."

"Right. Affirmative. *Ooh Rah.*" My small comfort and Peter's blood alcohol level propels him off the bed. Pacing with managerial enthusiasm, he affirms, "When you hit the wall, climb over. *Ooh Rah.* I just need to pre-think our shield time with the boss. *Ooh Rah. Ooh Rah. Ooh Rah.* Thank you, baby, for the battle rhythm. Pain is an illusion. *Ooh Rah.* Fear is the mind killer. *Ooh Rah.* That which does not kill me only serves—"

"Okay, I'm going to the bathroom."

"—to make me stronger. *Ooh Rah.* Bend like a reed—"

"You should probably change your clothes."

"—in the wind. *Ooh Rah.*"

"That's really annoying."

"There is no next time. *Ooh Rah.* It is now or never. *Ooh Rah.*"

* * *

79

*   *   *

In the adjoining bathroom, door slammed fast and hard on the motivational speech, I wonder what I'm doing with an avowed corporate citizen. Not a citizen of the world, not a citizen of a nation, Peter has chosen to be the citizen of a corporation.

Frankly, I don't like the nation state, or the corporate state, or even the state of humanity, and just as honestly, I know I've made a rather capitalist pact with the corporation to avoid a state of social assisted living. For all of that, at least Peter isn't a hypocrite.

He's a proud motto-spewing, logo-bearing inspirational shitstorm of a corporate citizen.

And I'm trailer trash that's joined the elite but is disappointed with the move.

Disappointed with the move, myself, and the duplicity of my life. It's my astrological nature, my two-faced double-dealing Gemini sign, addicted to pills so the two halves can tolerate the proximity of each other, but it's also my American right—yes, my damn American right—to recreate myself in a capitalist meritocracy. Don't judge me, it's the Ambien talking.

The promethazine is more of a socialist.

The zopiclone an anarchist.

And the methaqualone is only in it for the giggles.

Without them, I'd have to figure out who I am, with whom I stand, and for what, if anything, I might fight.

I'm not going to figure it out in the few minutes I have to get ready, not with the four of them rioting in my blood, and especially not with *Ooh Rah* chanting in the background.

Thankfully, experience has taught me Peter doesn't know five minutes' worth of leadership quotes. In three, he's quiet. In five, I emerge to find him in clean clothes and closing the flap to my shoulder bag. He hands it to me and takes both our carry-ons.

In the hall at the top of the stairs, he politely motions for me to go first.

I smile, say "Thank you," and put one foot forward. Then the Ambien makes the wallpaper undulate, and the zopiclone trips on the first step. The promethazine swears to god it's the rot in the balustrades shaking the handrail, and the methaqualone throws itself off twelve seemingly endless cliffs for the bottom.

I can't help but count each one as I fall: One, two, three, fourfuckfive, six, seven, skip eight, nine, ten—*Christ*—eleven—*help me*—twelve.

12

$1 + 2 = 3$

Sprawled on the foyer floor, I don't even have to check if anything is broken because three ensures the only injury is pride. Three keeps it in the ethereal, the spirit world, the realm of possibilities not yet realized. Everything up and until three is safe.

Sid Vicious obviously doesn't know his numerology and is unduly concerned. "Bozhe Moi," My God, "are you alive?" He reaches down to help, offering a tattooed hand.

Seeing the black widow leave the web of his fingers and crawl up his wrist, I recoil, and something like "Paukov hell i chërtov fury," Spiders in hell and the devil's fury, comes out of my mouth as I scramble to my knees.

"Uspokoysya." Calm down. Stroking the ink on the back of his hand, he explains, "She is just a harmless little heroin addiction."

I may be stunned by the fall and stupid from the drugs but I can still read the signs, and I don't want that poison anywhere near my skin.

He offers it anyway. "That had to hurt. If you want, she can take away the pain."

As I stagger to my feet assuring, "I feel nothing," Peter clangs to the bottom step with our luggage and asks in horror, "Jesus Christ, baby, what was that?"

"Oh, probably just a little omen of things to come." I try to make it sound almost pleasant.

He stares at me worried. "Did you hit your head?"

No, just jarred loose my soul, and Peter got an unintended glimpse of the superstitious thing.

Gathering my wits, my soul, and the bag of pharmaceuticals, I point toward the front door and insist, "We should go. You're meeting Konstantin."

The Hierophant

Alone in the back of the Jaguar, we wait for the Zomanov Pakhan. Peter looks over the yard filled with cars and Bratva, and says, "Christ, it was bright out there."

Relieved to be hidden behind the dark tint of the windows and no longer under the scrutiny of the brothers, he sinks into the seat and drops his head into his hands. He wants to know: "How long does it take Tylenol to work?"

"Maybe thirty minutes."

Squeezing his temples, he asks, "So I've got to live with this pain for another twenty minutes?"

$30 - 20 = 10 = 1$: *Something momentous has been initiated.*

My muddled brain starts processing the numbers and what they mean in numerology compared to what they mean in this moment. This moment and also ten minutes ago...

Something happened ten minutes ago.

Oh dear.

"Peter, did you take Tylenol from my bag?"

"Two. Maybe I should take another two."

$2 + 2 = 4$

Four would definitely bring the situation out of the ethereal and into the material.

"You don't need four." I don't need four. No one needs four right now.

And the numbers are changing. What's still on the table is ten, which is one, but unknown is what suit of two we are dealing with. Tylenol would be nice, but as you may remember, and Peter never knew, in the Tylenol bottle are also methaqualone and Ambien.

Now, if you don't know what methaqualone is, that's a Quaalude, and if you've never taken Ambien, it's exactly like Salvador Dali redecorated your skull.

Neither is suitable for introductions, as neither will facilitate a good first impression, but given a choice, I'd rather Peter had swallowed two Quaaludes than one Ambien because people who stay awake on Ambien turn very fucking weird.

The primary reason Ambien parties have never gone mainstream is because nobody can remember a damn thing that happened. You just wake to the inexplicable: the walls graffitied in Oscar Wilde quotes, the cat half shaved, the car missing, and the palm plant from the lobby of the Holiday Inn is sitting on the couch in sunglasses and full Masonic gear: apron, sash, and collar.

If you want to avoid suicide, for god's sake, don't look at your text messages, and just go ahead and delete your entire Twitter account.

Whatever you got up to you'll be lucky to never know, but you'll catch glimpses of it in the weeks to come as Amazon continues to deliver boxes of roller skates and crossbows.

By comparison, methaqualone should be legal. This is more like you've taken six quick shots of Tequila, a bar of Xanax, and are huffing nitrous in a child's bouncy castle.

Sure, you're messed up, but you can still recognize your actions as an extension of your personality.

It's too early to know yet what Peter has consumed, but the emerging smile says Quaalude, and this alone gives me hope I can bluff us through first introductions. Never mind I'm also under the effects of methaqualone (and Ambien and zopiclone and promethazine, yeah, yeah, I know), but I've developed some immunity, even learned how to act straight so Peter would never accuse me of substance abuse.

Peter, on the other hand, is now giggling, and says, "That fucker is fat."

Konstantin is coming.

The driver gets in and starts the engine while the passenger slings an empty vodka bottle across the yard.

And there is no way I can spin fat as phat. Pretty hot and tempting, Konstantin is not.

No, as Peter points out, "He's a big fat fucker in a suit that cost more than the house he's leaving."

"Stay polite," I warn, because Konstantin doesn't strike me as the type to be amused by such observations.

I might be honest and confess that Peter has taken my sleeping pills unaware, but Russians tend to be unforgiving of men who can't handle their intoxicants. And I sure as hell am not about to admit to Peter that I just unintentionally ruffied him before his first meeting with Konstantin.

As the door beside me opens and the Zomanov Pakhan joins us, the ominous fall down the stairs plays heavily on my mind. For all the sleeping pills, it might as well have happened in a dream, and in a dream such accidents represent a reckless lack of control.

I wonder what the Devil has to do with it when next the Bull enters the car and sits beside Konstantin. Eyes focused directly ahead, he's staring at Peter with hate again.

Konstantin introduces him, "Demyan Zharkov, my translator."

Of course. It—and my second underestimation of the Bull—all makes sense now. Konstantin would not have allowed Peter alone with Volikov without a spy—which confirms Felix

85

doesn't speak English—and the only way to ensure Demyan didn't pass out like the passenger was to make him the driver. Beautiful. I wonder if Konstantin knows I drugged Felix with Volikov.

And now Peter as well.

Poor Peter, drunk and hung over, whacked out of his smiling skull by hypnotics, trying to shake Konstantin's hand but missing by a foot.

As Konstantin catches the wayward limb, Peter laughs it off and says, "Good to finally sit down and burn grass with you."

I open my mouth to translate, but Konstantin looks purposefully to Demyan.

Demyan says, "He would like to smoke marijuana."

"No, wait, *wait,* that is not—"

Peter says, "Let's start a conversation for blue-ocean opportunity."

And Demyan translates: "The ocean is blue. Let us about talk it."

Holding up a finger, I mumble, *"Umm..."* while Konstantin makes a face of confused but otherwise congenial acceptance.

The convoy of cars leaves the translator's house as Peter says, "We've got a SWAT team dedicated to handling every moving part of your business."

And Demyan tells Konstantin, "We have a heavily armed and militarized team of sharpshooters who will manage your delivery trucks."

Konstantin turns his head to consider this unexpected offer and then gives a curt nod of appreciation.

86

The Jaguar picks up speed, and Peters says, "I've been to the top of the strategic staircase on this, and the thinking up here is nothing but blue skies."

And Konstantin hears, "I have climbed the most important stairs, and I think the sky is blue."

Because Konstantin looks disconcerted, Peter makes an effort to focus. Taking a breath, he confides, "Level field play here, we're fully prepared to open our Kimono."

Demyan struggles with this but finally says, "We would like to... *undress* and play on the ground."

Konstantin's brows come together.

I rise above the sedatives to forcefully intercede. "Please forgive us these misunderstandings. Translations can be difficult, and while your assistant has made commendable efforts to express Peter's thoughts, to avoid further misunderstanding, please allow me to speak on behalf of Peter and M and H Enterprise."

Squeezing Peter's knee too hard, his head finally sags in my direction. I tell him what I've said, and he responds, "Good. Tell him we need to make a paradigm shift and we'll reengage from base."

I think I hear Demyan strangle a laugh into a joyous hiccup, and when I look, he silently mouths *Pizda s ušami.*

Because I'm *invested,* I transform business speak into something comprehensible: "Please allow us to start again."

Konstantin nods and gestures for Peter to continue.

Peter's eyes glaze. "The core competency of our mission—"

Core competency? Just what the fuck is that?

"—is to align our goals with the strategic direction of your business."

Holy gibbering Jesus.

Peter pauses for me to translate, and Konstantin is waiting.

I begin, "In Dostoevsky's *The Idiot*, the reader is introduced to a naïve prince."

Peter continues, "Since we were in diapers, we've served the manufacturing vertical..."

"As you undoubtedly know, the Prince spent his youth in a sanitarium..."

"... and now I'm going over the wall to bring this home."

"... and he immediately regrets leaving its safe confines."

Beside Konstantin, Demyan is delivering a slow and silent clap. Peter snaps back to the moment and smiles.

I need to pull it together so at least one of us makes sense, but then Peter says, "We've got the bleeding edge on industry."

The bleeding-fucking-edge. Because what good is a cutting edge if no one gets hurt? *Amirite?*

All the MBAs in the world can't dig us out of this hole, and a master's in Russian literature has only ensured we'll have a highfalutin *la-di-da* quote inscribed on the tombstone.

Not waiting for me to translate, Peter carries on, "We've got the best practice to deliver your company values."

I consider the possibility of crying. Perhaps I'll win Peter the timber account through sheer pity.

"As your prime equity partner, we'll deliver on our connectivity from day zero."

Tears, yes, I think tears are in order. I can feel them.

Demyan closes his eyes and shakes his head at what he's about to do. He says to me, "You owe me for this."

As Peter continues, "M and H Enterprise is no goat rodeo. We're value add," Demyan picks up from where I left off to tell Konstantin, "M and H Enterprise is no naïve prince. They are oligarchs."

And I ask, "Is that a favor?"

Peter says, "Penetration pricing will m-penetrate."

And Demyan translates, "Oligarchs who respect oligarchs."

"Really? This is you helping?"

"Ride with our pathfinders to oxygen-move the entire industry."

"They are ruthless capitalists who do business with ruthless industrialists."

"Oh, dear god."

"And you, Konstantin Zomanov, will impact every key indicator."

"And you, Konstantin Zomanov, are a monster of industry."

"We're going to die."

But Konstantin is suddenly pleased. *"Da! Da!* Finally, I hear the words that speak to my heart. *Da,* we are ruthless oligarchs! This is what is important: to take and to have. What is wrong with the man that will not?" And with that settled, Konstantin slams his hand flat on his knee to declare, "I like you!"

Peter is startled awake. Blinking back into some state of coherency, he has no idea what's just transpired or what it means that Konstantin is so pleased.

"He likes you," I offer.

But this is no surprise to Peter because everyone likes him. He's a damn likable guy, especially when he's not plastered on vodka and Quaaludes.

The Devil

It's a five-hour drive to Bereznik.

If it were three, it'd be harmless, and four would at least be stable, but five is problematic. Five is the start of dissension, separation, the first break in an otherwise solid wall. There are times when it's good, but this is not one of them.

The second Quaalude kicked in an hour ago, and Peter has been talking about his mother. Neck resting limp against the top of the seat, he slurs his memories to the roof, "And then there was the time when I was six. We went to Tiffany's and she stole a whole silver dinnerware set. All forty-eight pieces dumped right into her purse."

Demyan translates this to Konstantin as: "And this is why the Azart Corporation is crucial to finalizing the deal. Having procured grants from the Federal Forestry Agency, they alone have the funds to pay for the expansion, upgrade, and maintenance of the roads."

The Azart Corporation.

Neither Peter, nor I, nor anyone at Morris & Hugo has ever mentioned the Azart Corporation.

Azart: gambler's rush, daredevil's passion, thrill seeker's high. It doesn't translate succinctly, but it's something like the excitement you'd feel after pimp slapping a lion.

Konstantin wants to know: "How much do they want?"

Demyan asks Peter, "How old were you again?"

Peter sighs, "Six."

And Demyan tells Konstantin, "Thirty percent."

Me? Oh, I'm just counting the hours until we're offered to the bears of the Bereznik forest. Perhaps we'll be given the chance to play dead.

I can't get to my phone in the shoulder bag without drawing attention, so while Peter waxes lackadaisical, "The most ironic time was when she stole padlocks," I try to inconspicuously reach into his pocket and set his phone to record. But I'm no pickpocket so nothing about my groping is discreet.

Peter says, "If I'd known your interest, I'd have cut a hole in the pocket."

Sitting calmly forward, Demyan removes my hand, adds his own, and then deftly confiscates the phone.

To me, he says pointedly, "Peter lost this," and then, while tucking the lost phone away in his own jacket pocket, he tells Konstantin, "Every year, Azart can guarantee two kilometers of paved roads, another four kilometers of logging access, and a further quarter billion rubles in upgrades."

"Uh, Konstantin," I interrupt, "it might interest you—"

"Did you know Peter had his juvenile records sealed? He has enough arrests we could make him honorary brother."

And the first kompromat is down.

"F.Y.I.," Peter's head rolls sideways, "stealing money with a gun will get you twenty years. Stealing it with a pen: six months. Pen for the win."

"Depending on how you play cards," Demyan continues, "we might even give Peter ace of spades. Tattoo it right on his neck."

"Ooh, cards?" Peter sits upright. "I'll deal. Spades, was it?"

Konstantin glares at the three of us and demands, "Speak Russian. What are you saying?"

"Sibyl hoped we might stop so she could take pictures of the countryside."

Looking with skepticism at Demyan's pocket and Peter's unseen phone, Konstantin barks, "Chush' sobach'ya." Dog shit. A bit messier than bullshit.

"Yes," I smile to agree, "that is what Demyan said also, you cannot take pictures of this beautiful scenery with an HTC twenty megapixel camera. Now, for fear I will not heed his advice, he is afraid to leave me alone with it."

In the uncomfortable moments that follow, I remind myself that Konstantin is nearly seventy years old and rules a criminal empire. He's probably seen every game played with every innuendo known to man. He's not buying it. I know this, and Demyan knows it.

Demyan stares at me but speaks to Konstantin, "I am concerned she might capture something that should not be shared. These phones have many capabilities." The insinuation is heavy that I'm a devious cheat.

Konstantin doesn't miss this either. He gives Demyan a quick nod of commendation. *That's why you're my rising star.*

And Peter takes this moment to ponder aloud, "You know that warning, 'You'll either end up dead or in jail.' That honestly applies to everyone."

* * *

For infrequent users, the effects of Quaaludes last about six hours. This means Peter arrives in Bereznik relatively sober—relative at least to the first five hours. He'll never regain the memory of anything that passed during those hours, and his short- and long-term memory won't recover until he goes to sleep and resets his brain.

He won't remember telling us about his kleptomaniac mother.

He won't remember Demyan taking his phone.

And he won't remember his epiphany.

It's also quite unlikely he'll recall our arrival at Konstantin's country dacha. If dacha is what you'd call the turreted Disneyesque palace ahead. Even Gaudy might blush and call it a tad ostentatious.

It looks as obscenely new as Demyan's house looked dangerously decrepit.

Konstantin prompts me for a response, "Ah? Well? What do you think?"

"Enchanting." Then pointing to the stairs leading to the arched entryway, "I see the inspiration for the marble Maserati."

"You noticed?" He smiles with affection. "I brought it all in from Tuscany."

While Konstantin tells me about using a Halo helicopter and its military crew to haul pretty rocks from Italy, Demyan continues his discussion with Peter, "Unless Morris and Hugo can supply extra two billion rubles to guarantee immediate road works, Konstantin insists on partnership with Azart Corporation. Morris and Hugo can still have majority shares, but without voting rights."

"Gazump!" Peter says. "That's a recontextualization we'd not anticipated."

94

The return to corporate artifice is a reassuring sign of his recovery. Given a few hours of sleep, a couple hours of sobriety, and a selective recap of events, he'll know how to handle Demyan and the Azart Corporation.

And no doubt fear of this very possibility sends Demyan from the car to organize the day's continued festivities. "Move all forty cases into the kitchen. Put Peter in the blue room and Sibyl in the tower."

The Tower.

Even the most naïve, New Age, everything-is-positive readers of the Tarot have the sense to dread the Tower. If you're particularly attuned, you'll shuffle the cards and feel the dark threat shifting through the timeline, and you'll keep shuffling until you think it's buried in the past. But then cut the deck three times and what you buried might come to the surface. And unlike every other card, there is nothing that can make the Tower any less calamitous.

The Fortune card is generally favorable, but pair it with the Tower and you get burning Ferris wheels.

The Queen of Cups is the promise of love, but next to the Tower it involves rivers of blood.

The fortuitous Chariot becomes the second horseman of the Apocalypse, the Knight of Swords turns into a tornado filled with rusty nails, the Hermit commits suicide, and the Priestess poisons the city well.

It's just bad-on-bad with the Tower.

I might decline the tower room, but there's no reason to fight it now. The Devil put the card into play as soon as he said, or essentially said, "Put the Eye in the Tower." (You didn't think that was Tolkien's original idea, did you?)

95

And from the tower, I've got a pretty clear view of the events to come.

By the river is an outdoor living space with grill, adobe oven, and restaurant-styled kitchen. Recessed under a manmade hill is a sauna, and near the forest is a tactical shooting range with what appears to be spring-loaded targets. More than a dozen women in bikinis and six-inch heels rise from the recliners around the pool to greet the arriving Bratva, and just beyond the pool, servants in traditional uniforms fill the center of six picnic tables with shot glasses and plates of food.

Peter's not been allowed to sleep but is instead with Konstantin at the gate of a savannah-themed enclosure. It looks like Konstantin is trying to convince Peter to put his hand through the bars to pet the lion.

Luckily, the Quaaludes are in retreat and Peter seems reluctant.

This seems particularly wise because I can think of only one reason Elvis is leading a goat to their location. *Someone's hungry.*

Smelling the air, the goat offers a worried sounding *"Meh." Baa.*

The assembled Bratva fall hushed. In one slow synchronized movement, they turn their attention away from the women and focus it instead on the bleating goat, and then, like the lion's pride on a hunt, the intensity of their interest holds them deathly still.

If Peter succeeds on this trip, these are going to be our new friends.

I imagine Peter is thinking much the same thing at the moment. As he stares over his shoulder, I suspect I can detect the look of strained mental reckoning while he tries to figure out how exactly he's come to be where he is now.

Like the goat, he has no easy escape, but I do. I turn away from the window and the scene about to unfold, and I'm not entirely surprised to find the Devil at my door.

*　*　*

The Devil smokes Sobranie Black. Standing at the threshold, Demyan cups the end of the cigarette against phantom wind and raises a disposable lighter to the tip.

While the flame ignites the tobacco, I read the inscription on the inside of his forearm: то что нас не убивает нас не интересует.

"That which cannot kill us does not interest us."

Exhaling poison, he explains, "Nice sentiment shared by thieves and Bratva." Waving away both the smoke and the idea, he gestures to the six narrow windows that circle the room. When his attention comes to the one overlooking the lion's pen, he says, "I thought you would appreciate view."

I ignore his oblique remark to complain, "This arrangement is going to prove inconvenient for Peter."

"Peter does not interest me."

"I do, though?"

"You could."

"Think I could kill you?"

He slowly considers the cigarette before his eyes stray down his arm to the relevant tattoo. He says, "Women have been killing men since start of civilization. For women, men will die in prison. Men will die in business, in traffic, in vain.

Every day, thousands murder own soul for career. Men will risk anything and sacrifice everything for women."

"So, what is her name?"

"Whose?"

"The woman for who you're risking death by involving the Azart Corporation."

"For now, she is just idea. Man needs money and power before he acquires mate. His value determines what is on offer."

"I see you're not a big fan of romance."

"Not true. Prison libraries have limited material, and officials think it very funny to stock shelves with romance. Romance books teach me everything about women."

"That is utterly horrifying."

"Women are simple, but there is something that confuses me. They want rich and powerful men, but they also want to be only thing he thinks about. I do not know how this is possible."

Shaking my head in dismay, I mutter, "I don't know whether to try and save you or not."

"Men do not need to be saved. It is women who want to be saved."

"..."

I close my mouth and try again. "..."

But my entire brain is overwritten with an ellipsis.

Six years of study and everything I know about life, literature, and relationships is erased and replaced with periods of ellipsis.

...

It seems impossible, but Demyan is right. Romantic literature is a testament to how much women longed to be saved, but free the woman of fiction and it is she who routinely saves the man; and yet, if Demyan's earnest statement is true, men themselves do not wish to be saved.

...

The paradigm shifts. Core competency collapses. Reality demands recontextualization.

I wonder what Demyan's favorite book is.

I wonder if he's had sex with a man.

I wonder how the goat is doing.

The Devil moves farther into the Tower, bringing with him smoke and ash and doubt. Red embers flare on the black cigarette as he opens a window. Softly, so his voice doesn't carry over the grounds, he says, "Come here. Look at this."

Standing beside him, he points across the front of the house, past the parked cars that brought us here, beyond the granite drive and the gilded gate, and into the thousands of miles of woods that surround Konstantin's modern castle.

"All this money and how does he use it? He builds playhouse. He swore oath to thieves to put them before all others. He swore to have no home other than prison. He swore to provide their needs as his own, but rather than improve thieves' lives, he decorates weekend dacha with gold."

I notice his body temperature is higher than mine. He smells of tobacco and rage. His lips audibly part as he brings the cigarette to his mouth, and as he inhales, there's a catch in his breath that's sensual; the exhale is even more so. He's tense and riled and dangerous, and I'm acutely aware of him. And he's done this deliberately. He's called me to stand beside him for the very effect it has.

If I were the careful, devoted type, I'd back away.

And I do consider it.

But then he says, "I need from you cooperation. I would prefer you give willingly."

Prefer. The veiled threat is too provocative to ignore. It's reckless. It's thrilling. It's *azart.*

It occurs to me: "The Azart Corporation is yours."

Before he can conceal his enjoyment, a fiendish grin confirms it. He ducks his head, pulls on the cigarette, and wrestles his face back into some fashion of austere. For the moment, I suspect his amusement is too close to the surface to risk looking at me. Instead, he points farther north and says, "Forest lease is three million hectares—like size of Belgium. This could produce billion rubles a year."

"And you're already a trillionaire?"

As though I've not registered a single complaint he's made against Konstantin, he glares at me with indignation.

"Then how are you going to fund the roads for something the size of Belgium?"

"Federal Forestry Agency was provided fifty billion to modernize industry."

"And you've been granted some of it?"

He nods.

"How did you get it?"

"Normal way: bribes and favors."

"And the money for the bribes came from...?"

"Same place as favors."

"Vory v zakone." Thieves in law.

"Ya vor." I am thief.

100

He's a thief that reads the classics, a convict who's only a few definite and indefinite articles away from perfecting English, a career criminal who undoubtedly controls an offshore corporation with a board of directors neither Konstantin nor Volikov can trace back to him, through which he's procured billions in grants and by which he intends to accumulate more. It's not intentional, but as I process this, I find myself shaking my head *No*.

"You doubt me?"

"How many years were you in jail?"

"I show you." Flicking the gold filter of the Sobranie across the rooftop, he closes the window and pulls me with him to the center of the room.

I'm not even surprised this time when the shirt comes off.

"I was sixteen first time I went to prison. That was seventeen years ago." Pointing to his left shoulder and the rose wrapped in barbed wire, he says, "This means I turned eighteen in jail." He offers me his fists. "Crosses are for time spent in solitary."

Six knuckles bear the emblem.

He flips his right hand to show me the inscription on the forearm: вор во́ ра кр́ оет.

Vor vora kroyet. A thief covers another thief.

"Thief should do anything to protect another thief. This includes going home."

"By home, you mean jail?"

Nodding, he looks down to his abdomen where a cathedral similar to Red Square's Saint Basil is inked over his stomach. "Every spire is different stint."

I really shouldn't, but I reach out to trace each dome with my finger. Five spires cover six well-defined muscles.

"How long have you been out?"

"Ten months."

Stepping back, I shake my head *No* again. "You want my cooperation but all evidence suggests—" *How to say this tactfully?* "—you suffer a high rate of failure."

"You do not understand. Ya vor v zakone." I am thief in law. "First time I was stupid, but every arrest after was deliberate. You cannot be crowned thief unless you do time. More time, more chances for promotion. For wealthy silovik, education leads to connections, but for someone like me, jail is best university. I have ten arrests, five convictions, and more trials than I can count, but I earned my degree, and it gives me permanent tenure with Bratva. It was not failure, it was enrollment."

"Nice. What's the retirement package?"

"It is what I make it. What is yours?" His face is hard with condemnation. "You plan to accept what others offer Peter?"

Said like that, it does sound rather contemptible.

His judgmental tone turns harsher. "Why do you not earn it?"

Because, to make money with a degree in Russian literature requires a doctorate and I barely managed a master's. I'm hoping Demyan's question is rhetorical so I don't have to admit that aloud, but time stretches into an uncomfortable silence while I stare at the floor.

"Work with me once and I will give you more money than you will ever see from Peter."

My expression turns to the amused side of skeptical.

102

"Ya vor v zakone," he says. "It is not profession, it is title. We have laws. We have codes. We pay all debts."

"You're loyal?"

"I am loyal."

"But you're asking for a difficult betrayal."

"When is marriage?"

"At the end of next month."

"You read Aleksandr Solzhenitsyn?"

"*The Gulag Archipelago*." I can't keep the bitter smile from my lips. "I already know what you're going to say."

"Then say it."

"Only those who decline to scramble up the career ladder are interesting as humans. Nothing is more boring than a man with a career."

"Take my money. End your engagement."

* * *

Turgenev—novelist and playwright, Russia's original nihilist, fomenter of the Russian Revolution—is tattooed on Demyan's back: Возьмите для себя, что вы можете и не исключено другими.

Take for yourself what you can and do not be ruled by others.

As if that two-part maxim is not enough to consider, here's something else: all tattoos inked in Russia's prisons must first be approved by the ruling thieves.

It's not only the stars on Demyan's knees that prove he's worthy to wear Turgenev, but his bold plan to steal from Konstantin further supports it.

He walks along Turgenev's cliffs with fearless abandon.

No two ways about it, it's attractive.

There is to it a reckless temerity that's enviable.

It's devil-may-care.

It's Demyan.

About as far removed from the stability of the Prince of Coins as Greenwich from any trailer park.

But Demyan's favorite Turgenev quote is a hard one to embrace. *Take for yourself what you can* is simple survival, and easy enough to accept; it's the last part that sticks: *Do not be ruled by others.*

More than just assuming responsibility for one's own fate, it's the rejection of oversight, guidance, and direction, a rejection of compromise, of societal mores, government laws, and religious doctrine, of all beliefs and institutions that have not been reasoned by the holder to be fit. It is to denounce all authority. To think for oneself. To go it alone.

And it is alluring.

At this particular moment, with marriage impending to a man I don't respect for status I don't deserve, it's more than alluring; it's azart.

The Universe

In the hocus-pocus cookbook of fortune-telling, the use of color as a predictor of personality is at the front with umbrella cocktails and toothpick appetizers. No one mistakes it for a meal, but the colors you choose can still tell a lot about you.

Take, for instance, red.

If you're wearing red, I might assume you want attention. If you're a woman, I might also assume you're ovulating. Attention for you might involve sex, love, or a baby.

If your living space is red, the matter moves from the body to the mind. Not to alarm, but there's a high chance your psychological profile will register abnormal on the psychotic scale. Not a serial killer, mind you, just more comfortable with aberrant ideas than most of your neighbors.

If your car is red, this clearly means you want people to *think* you're dangerous. And maybe you are. But you're probably not.

Based on color, I undoubtedly know more about Konstantin's interior decorator than Konstantin himself, but assuming he signed off on the gold color scheme, it's safe to assume he doesn't really trust his wealth. He doesn't feel rich. He feels like a fraud. And the bedazzling décor is meant to convince both himself and others of his success.

Leaving the tower, crossing the foyer, and entering the main hall, I'm left with little doubt of his worth.

The presiding style is Louis XIV. Everything—from the fittings to the moldings to the furniture—is carved and gilded. Gold tassels hang from gold rope around heavy gold drapes fringed in gold cord. Gold clings to the ceiling in ornate plasters. It drips from the chandeliers as garland. It accents the floors and overwhelms the walls. The armchairs, the sofas, the statues of the Virgin Mary, the paintings of the Baby Jesus, the tapestry of Saint John's ascension, and the fountain of Satan's defeat, every knickknack, every light switch, hinge, and door handle is gold.

If the Vatican were to swallow Versailles and a truckload of Goldschläger, this is exactly what it would vomit.

It doesn't surprise me the Bratva are outside. Inside is not a place many would feel comfortable. But in the vaulted living room, Volikov sits on an overstuffed sofa reading a tablet while Isaak has somehow managed to fall asleep in the hard arms of a Baroque throne.

The noon sun glints off the gilded mirrors causing refractions to bound mercilessly between the windows and marble floor. I enter the room squinting against the glare to ask Volikov, "Have you seen Peter?"

Shaking off the opiate nods, Isaak answers, "He is with Konstantin and crew at the pool."

"Odd thing"—Volikov looks at me from the top of his eyes—"Demyan arrived with his shirt off."

Isaak chuckles with the memory. "The Bratva, being what they are, took it as a challenge, and next thing you know, everyone is stripping to naked. Even Konstantin showed off his stars. Maksim and I could not hope to compete, so here we are, hiding inside like old gray bureaucrats."

Laying down the tablet, Volikov says, "I must compliment your fiancé. With all the brothers proving their lawless worth, he did not hesitate to show he has no obvious criminal past." Casually, he adds, "I heard you had a private chat with Demyan today."

"Did you?"

106

"Be careful with him, he is an idealist."

"You make it sound like a mental disorder."

"In his position, it is. Like the worst of your American Mafia, he romanticizes the institution. Konstantin is successful because he is a realist. What Demyan cannot bear to accept is the thief in law of his imagination has not existed since the sixties, when the State made it a capital offense to be part of a gang. Do you think Demyan would die for his beliefs?"

I'm thinking *Da,* but I go with: "Hard to tell."

"He thinks he is part of a noble tradition because he looks around and the only thieves in Konstantin's family, besides the obvious Pakhan himself, are Felix and Oleg—you would have noticed Oleg for the polar bear on his head—but these days practically anyone can join the thieves. A few million rubles and I could have Isaak crowned a thief."

"But not yourself?"

He dips his head and concedes, "They do have their limits."

"Enough gold could get me crowned," Isaak confirms, "but the guild would be looking for any reason to take the crown, and whatever tattoo they gave, off with a brick. It is not an honor many wish to suffer."

Volikov's sideways glance is a warning to Isaak against further contradiction. To me, he gestures to the seat across from him and says, "Sit. Peter has Demyan. He does not need you."

That's highly debatable. But, as most of the arguments support Volikov's statement, I sit.

He says, "Tell me about the Azart Corporation."

I should not have sat.

Following my gaze to the French doors that lead to the western gallery, the conservatory, and eventually to Peter outside, he says, "Do not be in a hurry to leave."

"Or a hurry to reply," Isaak adds whimsically.

As the previous sideways glance was far too subtle, Volikov turns full in his seat to put Isaak under a venomous stare.

"What?" Isaak shrugs. "You know this proverb: Never hurry to reply, but hurry to listen."

Like the motto for the FSB. But I'm not brave enough to actually say it. Instead, I try to shift the topic by asking, "What do you think about the lion outside?"

"Completely harmless. We removed his fangs and claws years ago."

As my expression turns to complete horror, Volikov corrects dryly, "Oh, you mean the lion in the cage. Still red in tooth and claw."

"But not in spirit." Isaak sighs. "With or without fangs, the lion's share is always too big."

"And the pride grows larger every day. What I would like to know is if the Azart Corporation is another mouth to feed, or a vulture circling for scraps."

"Well," I mumble, "your concern was the roads, and the Azart Corporation does offer a solution."

"At what cost?"

"As I understand, thirty percent."

Isaak's pupils dilate like an anime character, and Volikov erupts with *"Kak by ne tak!"*

Literally: As if not so. It's something you might shout when you're so overcome with rage you can't decide whether to exclaim *As if, Not Likely,* or *So not going to happen,* so you splutter a bit of each in one disbelieving interjection.

Recovering slightly, Volikov demands, "What did Konstantin say to this?"

"It might be better to ask Peter. Let me go get him."

"Call him."

"I... uh..."—look myself over—"don't have my phone."

"Use mine."

"Right. Thank you." Taking the offered phone, I heft it a couple times in my hand to appreciate the weight. "Is this a satellite cell?"

"Of course."

"Yes, of course it is. Why would it not be?"

"When you are in the woods with wolves, you learn to howl. *Or,* you could use a satellite phone."

"A very modern proverb." Handing the heavy thing back, I say, "Peter doesn't have his phone on him either."

Losing patience, he draws out the question: "And why would he not?"

"He... uh... lost it. Yes, he lost it. Probably in the woods last night."

Volikov moves an unspoken sentence around his mouth and seems to decide it would be easier to just swallow it than question it. "Isaak," he snaps. "Go find Peter. And *only* Peter."

The Hanged Man

As Isaak returns with Peter, Volikov is finishing his lesson on the thieves. "Because every thief must spend time in jail, it follows that every thief has been caught. This requirement ensures every thief is either careless or stupid. Of course, some are unlucky, but the average is on stupidity. For the rank and file, this is not necessarily bad, but the problem with the thieves' hierarchy is the more times a member is caught, the higher he goes through the ranks. The most incompetent among them are constantly promoted. You understand what this means? The thieves in law are run by court-appointed idiots."

For a moment, it appears Volikov might actually chuckle, but the grin that threatens to curl his lips is instead wrenched into a painfully fake smile at the sound of Peter's voice.

"Volikov, my man, glad to see you back at the keyboard."

I'm not about to remind Volikov that he went AFK with Felix after swallowing an aspirin. I'd rather Peter had said, "I am glad you sent for me."

"Yes," Volikov agrees, "we have much to discuss."

"Like the destructuralization of the blueprint."

"Not only the change in agreement, but we should also resolve the issue of the roads as well."

Settling into the gilded chair beside me, Peter takes a moment to look around the room and comment, "R backslash Room Porn. R Russian Immersion. R Overkill. Pick a subreddit, baby, and for maximum karma be sure to include that hideous thing in the corner. Have you ever seen that many doors or drawers on a cabinet? R What's In This Thing?"

Volikov interrupts his ogling to say, "Peter, I want to think of you as my friend."

"Not just your friend but your partner."

"It is your friendship I want, Peter."

"You are top of my BFF list."

"But friends work for the benefit of friends, Peter, not just themselves."

"Only rust works more tirelessly than me."

"Very good to know, Peter, because as my friend I would like you to show me the same generosity you provided yourself in the H2Y0 deal."

Peter opens his mouth to reply but stops short.

"I particularly enjoyed how you allocated funds in the advertising campaign. Very creative."

Closing his mouth, Peter stops smiling, stops breathing, stops moving. Seconds pass.

"What was the account you managed before H2Y0? Remind me, Peter."

Being the translator, Peter looks to me as though I'm the one toying with him.

"You have managed so many accounts, I know it is hard to keep track, but this one was more interesting than most."

Looking back to Volikov, Peter says nothing.

"It had that very, *very* large manufacturing budget."

Deathly still, Peter stares ahead.

"*Hmmm,* I'm trying to think... what was the name of that account you managed? Isaak, do you remember?'

"The Logstein account."

"Yes, *the Logstein account.*"

Peter is now ashen, and I'm feeling pretty certain the second kompromat is in play.

"Strange to pay such inflated manufacturing costs, but then, who really understands these Chinese agreements?"

With a desperately hopeful expression, Peter shrugs.

"Well, of course, we Russians do, but we did teach them the system."

Peter nods dismally.

"I find Peter's silence disquieting. Sibyl, have you been delivering my words exactly?"

Yes, and I translate that exactly too.

When Peter finally speaks, it's to say, "Baby, I want you to go upstairs and lock the door."

"No, I'm not leaving you alone with him."

"Baby... *I've done things.*"

"Clearly evident."

"I don't want you involved."

"It's a bit late for that."

"It's never too late."

"Yes, Peter, sometimes it is too late. You're in Russia. You don't speak the language. You're in the middle of a business deal with the mob and the government. It has never been so late."

Volikov's tone is sardonic. "Perhaps you two would like some time alone to—"

"*Shut-the-flibbertigibbet-up,*" Peter snarls.

I open my mouth to speak, but Peter snaps, "For fuck's sake, baby, he doesn't need that translated." Then glaring at Volikov, he adds, "Some things are universally understood."

Raising both hands in a sign of *Take all the time you need,* Volikov sits back to wait.

"Baby, I'm serious, go upstairs and lock the door."

"Peter," I try to match his severity, "dialogue is the only way to resolve this. You're stuck with me. It's either me or Demyan, and I promise you, you don't want Demyan."

"Richard Branson's Virgin ass!" Peter swears. After a moment's struggle for composure, he says, "All right, baby, we're going to do this, but you translate exactly. I mean it, baby, don't fuck with my words. Understand?"

Hand raised, I swear a silent oath to translate verbatim. It's not a hard promise to keep, not when the language of rage is devoted to clarity.

*　*　*

Neologism is out. Traditionalism is in.

Back straight, eyes hard, Peter says, "Mr. Volikov, succinctly, what do you want?"

"I want you to be my friend."

"Fuck you. What do you want?"

"If you cannot offer friendship, Peter, how can I be certain of your loyalty in business?"

"Extortion, Mr. Volikov. When loyalties waver, extortion prevails."

Tapping a thoughtful finger against the upholstery, Volikov says, "Perhaps I misjudged you."

"Well, *fuck-a-doodle-doo.*"

And don't think I can't translate fuck-a-doodle-doo into Russian. With the same flippancy as Peter, I say, *"Yebukoo-kah-re-koo."*

Volikov responds with disappointment, "Peter."

"What do you want?"

"First, the Azart Corporation."

Peter's eyelids droop in bored contempt.

"This thirty-percent ploy is merely an attempt to secure half."

"You're a genius."

"Even fifteen percent is too much."

"For the capital they're offering, ten percent is sufficient to keep them onboard."

"Agreed."

"Perfect."

"Wonderful," Isaak says.

Things are indeed going rather well, considering each thinks the other will pay for the roads for an extra ten percent, but then Volikov says, "Morris and Hugo will have to forfeit voting rights to maintain majority shares."

"Not going to happen."

"Yes, Peter, it will, and you are here to ensure it. Thankfully, for you, we are friends so Morris and Hugo will never learn of your previous indiscretions."

Peter silently considers it before coming to the conclusion, "They'll never agree."

115

"What need do they have for voting rights?" **Isaak asks.** "They do not understand Russian business. They should be happy to take their profit and focus their time on American business."

For a moment, Peter's mouth hangs open and then he deadpans, "Yeah, hoss, that's exactly how I'll sell it too."

Volikov calmly insists, "You will know what to say."

"I'll just tell them my candied-coated nuts were too sweet for you to resist."

I don't exactly know how to phrase that so I put Turgenev in the driver's seat and we go a little off-road in translation: "I want ten of your voting shares in Sibyl's name."

Amused, Volikov nods thoughtfully, and Peter nods back.

Volikov says, "So we understand each other: There are sixty-one voting shares. I own twenty-two and Isaak eleven. Konstantin has eighteen and Azart is granted ten. Giving Sibyl ten of our shares has the potential to give Konstantin voting majority. Whose friend are you, Peter?"

The shifty Turgenev translates that to Peter as: "You were granted legal authority to sign on Morris and Hugo's behalf. You need not tell them anything until the deal is complete."

Peter replies, "This deal is from the bottom of the deck."

To Volikov, the nihilist Turgenev repeats, "I want ten voting shares in Sibyl's name."

Volikov says, "She can have one of Isaak's."

Thinking Volikov said, "The deal is on the table," Peter responds, "And the dealer just dealt himself six aces from a standard deck."

Badass Turgenev maintains, "Ten voting shares."

Volikov counters, "Two of Isaak's."

Isaak mutters, *"Ummm..."*

Peter is told Volikov said, "Only half are mine," so he screeches, "Who's responsible for the rest?"

To Volikov, Turgenev responds from my mouth, "Ten."

"Isaak gives three. End of discussion!"

And in all the circles of confusion, Turgenev passes out leaving me to translate that last bit exactly.

Adjustment

Studies in neuroscience show our decisions are made moments before the conscious mind is even aware a choice needs to be made and everything that happens after is merely the mental wrangling of the troubled conscience trying to justify the subsequent actions. It's a solid argument against free will.

And, at times like these, any defense against self-determination is comforting.

Never mind that the absence of free will practically validates prophesy, fate, and divinity, and therefore, by extension, offers a certain legitimacy, and perhaps even dignity, to fortune-telling; the greater solace at this moment is that without free will I might not be entirely responsible for the events about to unfold.

I could say it was all in the cards and destined to happen.

That the decision to break my sworn oath was assured before I gave it.

That the choice to help Demyan was guaranteed from the start.

And backstabbing Peter is simply prophesy realized.

I mean, if you give even a passing nod to astrology, you can't very well believe in free will, now can you?

Not that free will stands up very well against science either.

Then religion kicks it right in the face.

And the Problem of Evil is just Christianity gratuitously burning it at the stake while simultaneously insisting it's God's

Will (omnipotent and benevolent) and also man's inherent nature (limited and evil).

So, let's set the notion of free will aside for the moment. The fates are at work. Consider this Dostoyevsky, where all seemingly insignificant misfortunes lead to one inevitable catastrophe.

Think of this as the Tarot, consulted mostly when one is already assured of the worst.

Or the old art of chiromancy: In Peter's palm is the promise of betrayal. I hold his hand in my lap and try to cover the looming turmoil in his love life, but I know it's there.

I know every line by heart, both the paths of his subconscious mind in the left hand and his conscious in the right. The major lines are strong, well-defined channels in his skin. Lines you'd find on an Earth sign, the Prince of Coins, a Taurus. There's no misinterpreting lines like these. But they are all—each and every one of them—broken.

Every line is split by duplicity and chance.

Strong and enthusiastic, his lifeline circles around the base of his thumb, but it's cracked twice at the start, once in the middle, and again at the end. His life will have many turns of fortune.

His heart line begins covered in tiny X's (probably his mother), and then there's the break and bold X that marks *the big betrayal* (probably me), which leads to a life of distrust.

His fate line is a choppy river ripped apart by events far outside his control.

Luckily, though, the head line is short: he won't spend much time dwelling on it.

He is not, however, entirely a victim of providence. He's played his part.

In his room on the second floor, he explains, "I'm just guilty of a little renumeration."

"Do you mean remuneration?"

"No, it's renumeration. Like when you negatively renumerate staff salary during a budget contraction. Or you make a positive renumeration on your expense account. Or a creative renumeration on your tax return. Renumeration, Sibyl. You're not this weak in Russian, are you?"

"So, what did you renumerate?"

"A few business accounts."

"I think the word you're looking for is embezzlement. That's *khishcheniye* in Russian. There's also *krazha* for theft and *moshennichestvo* for fraud."

"All really harsh sounding words."

"Fine, we'll call it innovative renumeration."

"Exactly, baby, *exactly*. I knew you'd log on."

"What happens if Morris or Hugo find out?"

"Whoa now, stop driving beyond the headlights."

"Huh?"

"You know, like, let's not get ahead of ourselves."

"Oh, okay."

"What hits the optic nerve is Maksim Volikov."

"Right."

"And what kind of Kabuki dance I'll have to perform for Morris and Hugo to buy in on Maksim's starship proposal."

"So, what are you going to do?"

"Well, I have to make it work or we're ruined. And more is at stake than just this little renumeration problem. I have my own plans for the sawmill. I've already bought land in Bereznik and secured leases on the two Soviet factories there. I have backing for a flat-pack furniture factory, sort of a Russian IKEA, and another that makes prefab walls with contracts pending with the Berserkistans."

"The who?"

"You know, the crazy Stans: Uzbekistan, Turkmenistan, Tajikistan... there's like a dozen of them."

"You have contracts?"

"Baby, I'm the hidden stockholder behind Aijan. I've got offshore companies in the name of the Swedes, the Fins, the Germans, all the companies contracted to buy the first wave of surplus below market value."

"Oh."

"Now don't look like that. I'm sorry. I didn't want to bore you with the dull parts of business."

"Hardly dull."

"I know, right?" In the excitement, he forgets to be contrite. "We're talking big-game strats here. The unintended consequence of some of my board moves is what Mr. Volikov discovered."

"What's to be done?"

"I'll have to go deep diving and look for the answer in the RDB."

RDB?

"Rectal Data Base. Because I'm going to have to pull some serious shit out of my ass to make this work."

"Truly poetic."

"It's a real bag of snakes."

"It is."

"Well, this is no time to be disincentivized." He stands with purpose. "Might as well go see if I can leverage some influence off the big boys."

Lust

The big boys are in the backyard playing with fire and knives.

At the furthest of six picnic tables, the Mongolian with a Mohawk shoves one end of a paper napkin into a bottle of vodka and lights the other. He pretends to lob it at Felix two tables away, but the flame chokes in the neck of the bottle before Felix becomes aware of the joke.

At the nearest table, the Ken Doll is using a six-inch serrated hunting knife to cut the fringe off the Fat Man's jacket.

The Fat Man says, "Stop or I hold you down and fuck you."

"Who knows?" Johnny Rotten laughs. "He might like."

A woman at the table has a few doubts. "Something about the way he says it makes me think it will not be memorable for its agreeableness."

The Ken Doll cuts another tassel from the jacket.

Booming over the laughter, chatter, and swearing of all the tables, a deep voice bellows, "Lev!"

Lev?

Lion?

Lion!!!?

Both women and Bratva scramble under the tables. *Under the fucking tables.*

"Lev prishel!"

The lion has come!

!

When Russian gangsters fight each other for cover, I know it's time to run.

With a squeak of fear, I spin to flee but only manage to fall into Peter.

Peter, blissfully unaware—even a bit amused by the ruckus—holds one arm around my waist and spins us in a circle that goes nowhere.

The squeak of fear turns into a squeal of terror.

Peter smiles, strokes my hair, and questions, "Baby?"

"Lion! Lion! Lion!"

"The lion is tame," he assures.

While I struggle to get free of his grip, he pulls my head to his chest and comforts, *"Shhhh."*

The squeak turned squeal is now a muffled scream against his shoulder. Death is certain. It is not what I thought. I read the cards wrong. Death just meant death. And death by lion... *Where is the damned grenade launcher?*

A rowdy cry comes from behind—*They're being eaten alive*—and Peter chuckles. A forger, an embezzler, and now a psychopath as well?

It's too much to take in one day. My muscles shake. My knees go weak. My weight is only supported by Peter.

Peter is laughing uncontrollably.

He tells me, "You're missing it."

He tells me, "They're insane."

He tells me, "They're under the tables knocking back shots."

How very Russian, I want to reply, but it's just a whimper against his shirt.

126

Trying to wrench my face around, he asks, "What are they doing?"

"Is drinking game." Demyan's answer is as close as it is calm. "Is called Lion Has Come." Casually, he taps a shot glass against my fingers until I release the death grip on Peter's arm. He says, "Relax. The lion is still behind bars."

While I gulp vodka, Peter exclaims, "The fuck do you play it?"

"Ante up. When Konstantin calls 'lion has come,' you get under table and drink." From the bottle he carries, he refills the shot glass. "When Konstantin calls 'lion has gone,' you come out and ante up for next round. Last man able to crawl from under table wins money."

"I'd like to strap that on," Peter says, and I swallow another shot.

"You all right?"

"Fine in three." I offer the glass for refill.

"Pace your positive momentum there, baby."

Peter doesn't see me down the third because Konstantin shouts, "Lion has gone," and the area erupts with laughing Russians emerging from shelter.

"I save you place at table," Demyan tells Peter. "Sit with my friend, Alyona." He takes Peter's arm and directs him to the table with Felix and Elvis and the sleek back of something so dangerous there's a blade tattooed down the length of her spine. The sword's crossguard extends across her shoulders, and the placement of the handle... well, I assume that's something of a dare: anyone who hopes to weld this weapon will have to grab her by the neck.

Following Felix's nod of recognition, she turns and smiles at both Peter and Demyan, but the red on her upturned

127

lips is a ruse. Her mouth is no warmer than her eyes. She's cool, remote, unaffected.

"Alyona, this is friend Peter I tell you about. Take care of him."

"Is what I do, yes?" Her expression is high-dollar professional.

Peter looks back to me and says with concern, "Baby, I don't think you'll want to play this game. It's going to get intense."

"I think you're right. I'll be in the tower."

The Devil follows.

*   *   *

If I laid out a spread that showed the Devil and the Moon in the Tower, I'd scoop up all seventy-eight cards and bury them in salt until they found a better attitude.

Not just cards, but any instrument of magic can be cleaned with salt. Salt erases the energy that people and events project onto objects. Salt neutralizes the vibes. It wipes clean the board. It restores to factory settings.

Used correctly, salt can save us from fate.

Salt can ward off the future.

Salt can deliver free will.

Salt is more powerful than you ever imagined.

If used correctly.

I mean, it's all occult nonsense, but I'd still like fifty-five pounds of it brought to the tower.

Demyan brings vodka.

But then, I did bring the shot glass.

I don't know why because I was determined to stop at three. Remember, three is safe. Everything up and until three is still just a thought, an idea, a possibility not yet realized. And the Three of Cups is Abundance. A lovely place to stop.

At least until Demyan strides across the room, saying, "We talk business." Kicking back the ottoman from an armchair, he motions for me to sit and then knocks the ottoman close again to sit as well.

Taking the shot glass, he says, "Tell me what Volikov wants," and the Four of Cups is poured.

"He wants the Azart Corporation to pay for the roads."

Without actually smiling, Demyan's face shows pleasure. He assumes, "You accepted my proposal," and returns the glass to my hand.

The Four of Cups is Luxury.

If I drink it, we're out of the ethereal and into the material. Four is for real.

Running his knuckles over the inside of my knee, he says, "You will like business with me."

Four's not that bad. It's just one little fall from grace, and it *is* still stable. I'll stop after four.

He takes the empty glass, fills it, says, "To thirty percent," and throws it back.

I mutter, "Not exactly." And he holds the vodka in his mouth. "More like ten."

It looks like he might spit or spew or possibly choke on the word that's drowning behind his lips.

"It's the highest either will go with neither being aware it isn't the other's idea."

129

He swallows to demand, *"Desyat?" Ten?*

"Why are you mad? Your investment is covered by grants."

"Is much less than expected."

"When you nationalize the expenditures but privatize the revenue, everything is profit. Ten percent of an expected billion is a hundred million more than zero."

"Rubles," he enunciates. "One hundred million *rubles,* not dollars. In US dollars, fifty rubles *is* less than zero."

He pours the fifth shot and downs it in an angry huff, and when he pours the next, I quickly drain it for mettle.

"That's not all," I say. "I want five of your ten voting shares."

I think he's about to hoof the ground to signal a deadly charge, but he's just hooking his foot around the chair to drag the two of us closer so he can ask the murderous question: "You want what?"

"F-Fiv—*our* voting shares."

"Four is it, now?" He yanks us closer.

"I—I could be good with three."

He can't haul the furniture any closer, so he wraps an arm around my waist to wrench me from the cushion. "Why you want voting shares?"

He's the Devil and he's wonderfully dangerous. I push against his chest for a distance I don't really want.

A breath away from touching skin, his mouth moves across my cheek to the ear. Lower now, he asks again, "Why you want voting shares?"

I keep the shot glass in my right hand, but with the left, I circle his hip to run my fingers under his shirt, along his

130

back, beneath the hooves of the bull, in the dirt with Turgenev, and after a moment, I quote from memory the creed on his back: "Take for yourself what you can and do not be ruled by others."

He exhales a slow breath of laughter, which turns into a growl of arousal.

Few know it, but the Devil rewards insurrection. After all, rebellion *is* the original sin, and he did conceive it.

Demyan holds the bottle to my mouth and offers the sixth shot. The last shot, the Five of Cups, was Disappointment, and we can't very well stop there, not when the Six of Cups is Pleasure and his lips are on my neck.

I drink long and lustful from Pleasure while shivers run my spine. My throat is still burning when I turn the bottle back on him, catch the lobe of his ear in my teeth, and make certain he drinks from the same cup as me.

I release his ear to whisper, "I want three of your voting shares."

"You're greedy."

"You promised me more money than I'd ever see from Peter."

He scoffs. "You have too high estimation of him."

"Without him, the Azart deal won't happen."

"He knows truth?"

"Your version of it."

"You didn't betray me."

"The price of my loyalty is three voting shares."

"I give you one." Then after a moment, he chuckles. "I don't want you having more balls than me."

"Two or it's off."

"You want two balls, you have mine," and he moves my hand to his groin.

"I will have yours. Two of yours." Then applying gentle pressure, "And maybe I'll take these as well."

Pulling me forward until I straddle his lap, he asks, "You always this much fun?"

"No, but you bring it out in me."

"This is what you bring out in me." I can feel him pressing hard against my pelvis.

He grabs the bottle from the floor and pours the seventh shot.

The Seven of Cups is Debauch.

And who doesn't want to drink to a bit of debauchery?

I down the shot with one hand while the other rips back the top button on his jeans.

The Seven of Cups is a chalice of poison that promises ecstasy but delivers regret.

Regret is for later. Right now, it's ecstasy. His hands are under my shirt unclasping my bra. His mouth is already tugging it away.

Running my hands up his sides and over his chest, I free him of his shirt.

To consume what it offers is to pursue false desires and sink into artificial security.

I pour his seventh shot into my mouth, and then, my mouth to his, I give him a taste of debauchery too.

The shot glass I toss over his shoulder, toward the mattress, and say, "Fuck me on the bed."

And Demyan—his voice a low rumble of need—demands, "Speak English."

"Govorit po-russki." Speak Russian

I unzip his pants as he rises from the ottoman, then slide my legs down his, taking his jeans and my feet to the floor.

It is pleasure corrupted.

"Mozhet byt' ya zastavlyu vas umolyat." Maybe I make you beg for it.

"My begging will lead to your pleading."

"Eskalatsiya? YA lyublyu eto." Escalation? I love it.

"Standard American-Russian relations."

"Dlya etogo ja xocú tebjá výjebat." For that I want to fuck you. But it could also mean, For that I plan to fuck you up.

Either way: "I hope you do."

"Kakaya tvoya fantaziya?" What is your fantasy?

"Whatever yours is."

His eyes narrow and he growls, "Togda davayte nachnem." Then let's get started.

Oh, god.

Hours later, the Devil has almost exhausted the Seven of Cups.

Swilling from this cup will lead to acts of depravity so obscene the conscious mind will reel away in shame, but still the drinker will not stop as the easiest way to soothe the humiliation is to drink again.

"Where's the vodka?" I fumble over the side of the bed and find it under Demyan's pants.

At this point, swilling straight from the bottle wouldn't seem crude, but the shot glass is beneath the sheets, digging into my ribs, so it's just as easy to extract it and pretend to be civilized.

The Eight of Cups is Indolence.

Demyan lights his last cigarette.

I drink, then pass him the full shot glass.

Dropping the empty packet on the floor, he pulls on the Sobranie and says, "We're going to have fun."

"I don't think I can handle any more fun today."

"That leaves all of night." He drinks with a smirk.

"Luckily, it won't arrive for another five days."

"Five days?"

"The White Nights end at the start of July."

"July, big month. Konstantin has birthday."

"Yes, July twenty-third." *The date of my wedding.* I spin the four carats around my finger and think, *I really should have stopped at four.*

But that seems so long ago it might be best to just carry on, maybe shoot for oblivion or circle back to one again. But the bottle is almost empty. Twirling the remnants around the bottom, I know there's only one shot left.

The Nine of Cups is Happiness.

I offer it to Demyan.

The Ten of Cups would have been Satiety, but we're a long way from there.

The Moon

I am the Moon. I have always been the Moon. In every reading, in every spread, no matter who shuffled or dealt or asked for guidance, if I'm going to appear, I show as the Moon.

Some men are terrified by the dark nature of the Moon, but not the Devil. The Devil is afraid of nothing he can fuck. And there's very little the Devil won't stick his dick in. He'll bugger the Priest, orgy with Art, and rape the shit out of Justice. The whole of the Universe is the only hole he won't try to fill.

But that still leaves twenty-one other divinities and sixteen nobles for him to ravish, possess, and molest.

I feel a little dirty. A little ashamed. A little wanting.

I feel... *good.*

Yes, I feel good. And alive and changed. Death is change. Death is always change. Silly of me to think it was the lion.

Konstantin is the lion.

He's the lion by right of astrology, the tiger by the Chinese Zodiac, and numerology and Western symbolism call him the cat with nine lives.

And he's a fat cat. Besides being the Pakhan, the reason he doesn't ante up to play Lion Has Come is because he's entirely too big to get under any table.

Instead, he's calling the shots, and based on the number of deposed, he's been somewhat restrained. From the tower window, I notice a woman face down in the grass, and three more sprawled indecent across the recliners. Four, including Alyona, are still in play, but the rest have opted to quit before any serious amount of dignity is lost. The men don't have that option. The men play until they can't.

The backyard party is now condensed to four tables. A few rubles are scattered on the wind, but the growing bulk of it is weighed down by ashtrays and plates of pickles and bread.

At table one, Peter is doing well, considering. Considering he hasn't slept. Considering he's not a full-time alcoholic. Considering he's not Russian. He's got one hand resting on Alyona's hilt, and he's wearing Felix's Armani slippers, but he's otherwise composed.

Across from him, Felix is barefoot and the red smoking jacket is somewhat askew, but even with the wild ember-throwing shake of his smoking hand, he's doing better than Elvis whose pompadour looks like a murder of crows trying to take flight from his head.

Beside table two, the Fat Man is down to his underwear. His skin is scratched bloody and raw from squirming through the rough boards of the picnic table, and his present solution is to pour a liter of olive oil over his body.

Two of the tattooed men are dipping bread in the hollow of his chest where his enviable breasts intersect with his belly, and four more are in tears watching it.

The Mongolian with a Mohawk struggles to hold James Dean's head flat to table three while the plastic Ken Doll draws a mustache on his upper lip with a Sharpie. A nearby blonde and redhead shake their heads in dismay.

Johnny Rotten leaves table three to join table four, which is in an uproar because Louis Vuitton is trying to get any one of the three women there to suck the pickle in his pants.

Tables five and six have become the repository for empty bottles, one nearly unconscious brunette, and the urine of the Strongman who is pissing in a jar.

136

Being a heroin junky, Sid Vicious isn't drinking but is lazily driving golf balls into the shooting range, and, just as bored, the lion is laid out spiritless on a rock. But miraculously the goat is still alive. Isaak is at the bars bottle-feeding it a six-pack. At first this strikes me as callous entertainment, but then I reconsider and think it might be the most compassionate thing I've seen in the past thirty hours. Why not be blissfully unaware when the lion eventually turns?

Four stories below, Demyan finally exits the house to rejoin the party. He's arrived too late to join the game, so instead he attends to the fallen. He hefts the unconscious woman from the grass and rests her on a poolside recliner. Covering the naked buttocks of the woman to her right with a towel, he then shifts the woman to the left onto her side so she doesn't choke on vomit. Unknown is whose puke is spreading through the pool, but Demyan directs one of the attending staff members to clean it.

Of any importance, only Volikov and the Polar Bear are unaccounted for.

I look back to where Konstantin is entertaining a buxom lady in a tiny sailor suit. A couch and table from the outside living space has been moved across the grass closer to the picnic tables, and the fat cat is lounging in the center with the squirming woman's foot shoved deep into his mouth.

To look at him you wouldn't think he's long for this life. He's aged, he's obese, and he's puffing so hard to breathe he's about to get his teeth kicked loose for tickling.

I figure his heart is pumping triple time to get the blood to every very extreme extremity, which really doesn't bear thinking about, not when it's safer to notice the fat on his stomach has his navel pushed a good twenty-four inches from other vital organs. His gold laden ring fingers are swollen past size 20, and his shirt is unbuttoned all the way back to the 70s.

There's no overlooking the man is huge. And old. And apparently horny. I suspect Viagra and an imminent heart attack.

Before he dies, I need to talk with him.

I need a few of his voting shares.

And I need to get them without either Demyan or Volikov suspecting.

But before descending the tower's spiral stairs—a dizzying prospect—I also need to stave off the impending alcohol crash. It's a good time for promethazine. And maybe a Quaalude. Then what I wouldn't give for cocaine.

Come on, you didn't think I was doing all this other shit without trying cocaine?

I already told you I was raised in the endless circuit of Renaissance fairs, a hive of users, abusers, and escapists of every ilk.

Trust me on this, everyone—from the ticket sellers to the archers—is high.

It's not unknown for the jousters to recover on ketamine, the pike men on codeine, and who doesn't know the barkers are blazed for days on meth? The jugglers regularly roll on X while the magicians trip on shrooms, but you'll be happy to hear the sword swallower only rages once on PCP.

Food vendors, crafters, my parents, all stoned out of their gourd.

I was taught to smoke weed in a potato by the Russian armorer. And then I learned how to drink, fuck, and read Cyrillic in chainmail.

138

Ah, the good old days of the Renaissance fairs, they made me what I am today: a fortune-telling Russki lover with a drug habit.

Shameful really. That's why I hide it from Peter, and also Peter's society-conscious parents, and Peter's presentation-is-everything employer, and Peter's wealthy friends, all raised on Connecticut's Gold Coast with summer yachts and trust funds. They'd no more understand my gypsy upbringing than recognize the full moon is opposite the sun, currently sextiling Mars, an alignment which makes Leo recklessly favorable to Gemini, something I really must go and take advantage of.

*　*　*

Walking on Quaaludes is not unlike walking on an inflatable raft, and the number of Quaaludes taken determines the swells in the ocean. Having taken only one, the water is calm but the floor is still rubber.

The grass extending across the back lawn seems to ripple underfoot.

From the various tables, laughter mingles with conversation and the occasional voice stands out.

"The woman could mangle firewood."

"Oy-yo." Oops.

"I think conversation with her is empty pizza, but later she sends me picture of pilótka."

Pilótka: military field cap, which looks surprisingly similar to a vagina.

Nearer the pool, I hear Johnny Rotten shout, "I have biggest dick here!"

"My dick in your mouth does not count," Felix calls back.

At table two, the Fat Man watches Peter sitting too close to Alyona, and says sardonically, "And the wolves are fed and the sheep are safe."

The rest of the table turns to stare. Then table three wonders what's happening and turns as well, and four can't resist joining in.

Standing beside Felix, Demyan explains the attention to Peter as: "They happy you come."

"It requires confident humility to embrace learning in public," Peter's voice rises to fill the space. "For the authentic dialogue, I thank you all for the invitation to your gracious space."

Alyona translates, "Peter is grateful for gracious space."

"Gracious space? The fuck is it?"

"Is like IKEA."

"Did someone get him coffee table?"

"I got no fucking coffee table. *He* gets coffee table and I must hold coffee in hand?"

"You do not need coffee table."

"I *need* a fucking coffee table."

"When you run the bald dude through your fist," i.e., masturbate, "as much as American, *then* you need free hand and get coffee table."

"He has two hands."

"Other is for *abrikosy*."

Abrikosy = apricots = testicles.

Demyan translates, "They thank you too."

It's 6:00 p.m. but the evening sun is still high in the sky. Squinting against the glare, I finally weave my way past the pool. Alyona sees me coming and twists her shoulder so Peter's hand drops from the crossguard tattooed across her back.

Another time under different circumstances and without the Quaalude, I might care, but at this moment, subverting her seduction of Peter doesn't serve me. I'd rather she have space to work, so I angle sharply away toward Konstantin. He still dominates the couch but is now deeply engrossed in exploring the woman's cleavage. It's not really the time to interrupt.

Unobtrusively, I take a chair at the edge of activity.

Demyan's face creases with worry.

To prevent his expression from twisting into full-blown suspicion, I turn my head west, past the grill, and watch Vicious as he continues to drive golf balls into the shooting range. He sinks a ball into the nearest pit and then another into the one beside it. Pulling three balls from the thirty-gallon bin at his side, he tees them all up. One after the other, he knocks turf and tees into the range's activation pillar while burying all three balls in a single faraway target.

Intent on watching Vicious and not arousing Demyan's mistrust, I only notice Alyona has taken the seat beside me when she asks, "Is first time in Russia?"

"I did all my summer courses here."

As though she's been caught in the wind—and not a Russian drinking game—wisps of hair fall from the bun on her head and soften her sharp features. From her sky-blue eyes to her grass-stained knees, she could not be more striking.

"What school?"

"Saint Petersburg State."

"Liberal Arts?"

"Yes."

She runs her hand over her neck as though her muscles are tense, but I suspect she's really wrapping her fingers around the grip, straightening her back, readying the blade that runs the length of her spine.

"You know, *this*"—her hand spreads out to encompass the scene before us—"this is not..."

I think she's going to say *me*.

This is not me.

But after a pause, she starts again with, "I have degree in economics, but I make more money doing *this.*"

"I have a degree in Russian literature, and I make no money at all. I suppose we're not that far apart."

"To educated whores, then." She lifts an imaginary shot and tosses it back. Before I can close my shocked mouth, she turns on me with eyes of fury and demands, "What? You won't drink with whores?"

"I... uh... I'm," *scared,* "more of a pill popper."

"Yes, you look the type."

"I'm sorry. I don't know why I just told you that."

"Because you have no friends here."

Brutal.

"Don't worry, is just fact. Like this." Again her hand sweeps across the scene, but this time she stops on Peter. "I

142

know you have terrible thoughts of me but is job with him, nothing more."

"Actually," *I cannot shut the hell up*, "I rather appreciate it. Your work will make what I have to do easier."

"Ah." Understanding instantly registers on her face. "Sorry to hear of it."

I look around for something to shove in my mouth: food, drink, more pills would be excellent at this point. It's not like it would surprise her.

From the table before Konstantin, she hands me a hunk of bread and says, "You're welcome." And then, "You're easy on the eyes," and a moment later, she adds, "... *to read.*" And she smirks.

It could be the Quaalude, but I think she might be friendly.

While I nibble on the crust, she gathers her tousled hair and rearranges it on the top of her head. It's still a beautiful mess when she gives up, crosses her hands and leaves them to rest over the pommel hidden on her scalp. She asks, "Why you end it with pretty Peter?"

"It was something I read. Do you know this quote, 'Take for yourself what you can and do not be ruled by others'?"

"Who does not know quote? Demyan likes to take shirt off." She almost rolls her eyes in contempt before adding, "Be careful with him."

"He's an idealist?"

"He's pervert."

A demented memory makes me smile, and she misreads my expression when I ask, "What can you tell me about Konstantin?"

"*Aha.*" She snaps the fingers of one hand. "You have your eyes on the big man?"

"Sort of. He wants you to seduce Peter for kompromat, yes?"

She shrugs and offers an impassive, "Eh."

"Or do you work for Volikov?"

"I *work* for money."

Her correction is so sharp I want to apologize, but for what offense I'm not entirely certain. The Quaalude, however, is still curious, and somewhat fearless, and, okay, stupid, so instead of expressing regret, I ask, "How much money?"

"More than you gain from Peter."

Or was it: "More than *you* gain from peter."

While I speculate on her English capacity for double entendre, she moves on to the rather cutting question, "I wonder, how stupid does girl have to be for man like Peter?"

I'm reduced to the ellipsis again. "..."

"I need to know. If I want *nice,* rich man, how stupid must I act?"

"..."

"You act stupid, yes?"

"Uh..."

"Is that how you do it? Do I make correct face? *Ulllhhh?*" She practically drools. "Is good, yes?"

"Like you were born to it."

"I try again. *Ulllhhh.* Maybe Peter will enjoy me because I remind him of you."

The Quaalude is certain. "You like me."

144

She looks across the lawn to Elvis throwing cigarette butts at Rotten, and sighs. "I like you more than anyone here. I very much tire of this job."

"But are you good at it?"

"The best." Her smile is equal parts bravado before indignity and absolute certainty she's right. "Why do you ask?"

"You say you work for money, and I need to buy a friend. Do you take Bitcoin?"

"I *love* Bitcoin."

The Emperor

Of course the Queen of Swords loves Bitcoin. Bitcoin is an idea that lives in the air, and this queen rules the air and all things intangible. Ethics, morality, and law, it's all much the same for her. Same with concepts such as jealously, hate, and love, she's quite above it, untouched by Earthly concerns. Not even the Devil can drag her down into the dirt.

Poor, dirty devil. The air, the heavens, and the emptiness of space are his undoing. He can't ground them, though he tries. He's trying now with Alyona, but after she whispered secrets of Peter in his ear, she kept herself just far enough away that his questions couldn't be heard if not shouted, and now, plagued with doubts unanswered, he lets her lead him away.

She's the best.

A real professional.

Worth every coin the Prince doesn't know he lost.

I suppose on the embezzling front Peter and I have something in common. Yes, well, don't fault me for not blatantly mentioning it earlier. It's not like it wasn't obvious. How do you think I pay for the pills?

Bitcoin and innovative domestic finance, that's how.

And I'm not done innovating. Once Demyan is off the field, I'm free to talk to Konstantin. And then, after I have a couple of his voting shares, I'm going after Isaak.

But first, the little sailor whose foot is covered in Konstantin's spit needs to set sail.

I figure she's looking for an excuse to dip it in the pool, so there's no opposition when I ask Konstantin, "Can we have a moment alone?"

After he calls, "Lev prishel!" and the party falls under the boards, he pats the now empty spot beside him.

The couch is large but still his knee, his thigh, and the fat of his upper arm press against my side. Peter would call this a *tactile situation*, because even the Russians would agree, things haven't been sticky since the 90s.

"Now we are free to talk, I am unsure how to begin."

"But you have something to tell, I know. You tried to tell me in the car. It has something to do with the Azart Corporation, yes?"

"Yes."

"I know the moment I hear this name, Azart, it is no good."

"Perhaps. But it could be turned to your benefit."

"Ah, but always at a price, yes? Well then, let me hear it: what is the cost?"

"Less than allowing Volikov to maintain voting majority."

He looks at me sideways before bellowing, "Lion has gone!"

While table two births the Fat Man in a puddle of oil, Peter belly crawls from table one and then reaches back under to drag out Felix, but it's table three that has our attention. With a rumbling growl, the table rises from the ground, tossing off detritus, and seems to be leaving the scene on skinny legs.

Johnny Rotten rolls as the table makes a quarter turn and bottles take flight, but Louis Vuitton is too slow to respond. The bench seat strikes him upside the head and sprawls him sideways.

Three women scream—*"Oooyyyaaahhh!" Aaarrrggghhh!*— and the goat screams back, *"Meh!" Baa!*

The women cover their heads against the rain of plates and pickles, and the goat tries to run but falls down drunk.

Under the table, the growl turns to a grunt as the weight is hefted onto the Strongman's shoulders. He makes another quarter turn, bringing the opposite end of the table back at Rotten's head.

Rolling again, Johnny swears, "Mne pokhuy." Fuck me.

The women scream, *"Oyah!"*

The goat bleats, *"Meh!"*

And the lion lifts his head.

When the table is tossed—*Bukh. Thunk.*—the drinkers cheer—*"Ura!" Yeah!*— and the lion yawns.

Konstantin, motioning to the action, asks, "You like to play?"

"I was never that good at drinking."

"But you like to play games?"

"I prefer not."

"Now is the time for little foxes to play. The lion is gone."

"But is he? The only time the lion leaves is to mark his territory or kill something. By that account, he is never really gone. Not really. Not safely."

149

He thoughtfully nods his head before saying, "It is good we understand each other."

As the redhead from table two vomits into the Strongman's piss jar (still on table five), the lion lazily stretches off his rock and notices the goat trying to clamber to his hooves, but for all the stability they offer, the goat's legs might as well be pasta. The lion is now decidedly interested. In a fast trot, he descends on the goat, and then, wrapping one big paw around its neck, he rolls with it to the ground.

The goat screams, *"Me~e~e~e~eh!"*

I invoke *Christ,* and Konstantin asks, "You have an idea to remove voting control from Maksim Volikov?"

"Me~e~e~eh!"

God in heaven.

"Me~e~e~eh!"

Don't think about it, don't think about, just get back to business and answer. "Yes, but to do it I need five of your voting shares."

"And I thought you understood me." He slowly fills his lungs with air and then fills the air with a roar, **"Lion has come!"**

"Jesus!"

"Me~e~eh!"

All lesser creatures dive for cover.

Into the echo of the roar, I quickly babble, "Right, okay, understood."

"Me~eh."

I'd like to sit upright again so it doesn't look like I'm cowering, but the Pakhan seems to have expanded. Pressed crooked against the arm of the couch, I try not to sound as terrified as the goat. "I honestly need one. One voting share and I can deliver Azart's vote. With my other six shares, I can guarantee you voting majority."

Gazing into the lion's pen, Konstantin is not particularly concerned with time, or the people under the tables, or the goat in the cat's embrace. He watches the lion run its tongue repeatedly down the length of the goat's spine, over and over, either savoring or grooming, it's hard to tell.

When the goat is down to a pathetic *"Meh,"* Konstantin finally asks, "If I give you one share and you do not deliver, tell me, little fox, what do you think will happen?"

"Probably nothing pleasant."

"Do you know about the time the lion played cards with the snake, the bull, and the vixen? The lion was dealing, and he warned the group, 'No cheating. I do not like cheating. If anyone cheats, she is going to get it right in her furry red face.'"

Fortune

The snake, the bull, and the lion have promised the vixen seven voting shares. This puts me in the coveted position of being able to swing a vote any direction I like.

I'd hoped for ten—ten is such a nice number—but the minimum required was seven.

You thinking lucky sevens? Wrong game. While sevens might be lucky in craps, they are *not* lucky in cards.

In my deck of cards, the sevens represent the lowest degradation of every element. And as Konstantin Imperiya is a timber company, the seven voting shares are represented by the Seven of Wands, Valor.

Oh sure, valor sounds heroic, but it's the hero's desperate last strike for victory, a dead man's jab, the sort of flailing maneuver that invites tragedy.

If I were the sort to believe in all this esoteric mumbo-jumbo, such an ominous warning would be enough to make me abandon the endeavor altogether.

Thankfully, though, I'm a skeptic. A bit superstitious, yes, but a disbeliever nonetheless.

And the rational thing to do at this moment is call in the lawyers and quickly get the shares dispersed.

It's the sort of thing Isaak would arrange.

With the Quaalude still whispering, *It's all totally cool*, I walk back across the rippling lawn for the conservatory and find Isaak sleeping upright on a cast-iron bench. At his back, two Bermuda palms almost touch the bougainvillea near the twenty-foot ceiling.

I take a cast-iron seat beside a bromeliad and across from Isaak, and then nosily adjust the orchid on the table between us.

If we were at the equator, like the surrounding environment suggests, the position of the sun would indicate it's about 2:00 p.m., but in Russia in June, it's just after seven. Still, anyway you look at it, it's a bit early for sleep. I consider rearranging the orchid again but Isaak is instead woken by the splash of a picnic table entering the pool.

He opens his eyes with a weary sigh and then looks a little spooked to find me smiling at him.

"So anyway," I begin as though he dropped off mid conversation, "if you would call the lawyers, we could have this whole deal wrapped up by midnight."

"And everybody goes home happy?" (Sneering opiate addicts are the Betty Davis drag queens of the drug world.)

"I suppose not. The final deal was not exactly in your favor."

"Always the same with Maksim: I toil and suffer, and he profits."

"He is not a very nice man, is he?"

"No, he is not."

"I *am* sorry. It was very unfair of him to take your shares. I wish I could help, but I do not understand business. I only translate."

"I speak English."

Well, fuck. "Does Volikov?"

"You are only alive because he doesn't."

"I suppose a thank-you is in order."

154

"I did consider..." And he looks far away while considering my death. *"But!"* He springs back to the moment with enthusiasm. "Because you recognize unfairness and express desire to help, I am sure we can keep you alive."

"Oh good."

"Do you know what I want more than anything?"

"To get back to sleep? I'll go now."

"I want Maksim Volikov in coffin."

"Please say you mean a Chevy Tahoe."

"I do not mean Chevy Tahoe."

"No, of course you don't."

Isaak's attention fades again into the distance. He might be listening to the violent splashing outside, or he might be straining to hear the gentle splatter of the nearby fountain where Adam, in glorious high-gloss gold, appears to be strangling Eve with Eden's most troublesome snake. The two conspirators are not faring well. Head wrenched back, Eve's open mouth is gurgling bubbles while looped tight around her neck the snake vomits water. Adam's mouth is also open, but his is twisted with rage, much like I suspect Johnny Rotten's mouth is twisted, so it appears Adam is bellowing, "Tebya ne ebut ti ne podmakhivai."

Rotten simply means, "Mind your own fucking business," but it's hard not to think Adam is being literal: You're not being fucked so don't wiggle your ass.

[In case you're wondering, the opposite of a euphemism is a dysphemism; and let's just be clear, no nation on Earth competes with Russia at dysphemisms.]

Isaak says, "I want Maksim buried under six feet of shit, under sea of shit, under sky of shit with black stars of shit in galaxy of shit."

155

"Wow. That's a lot of shit. I don't know where to get that much shit. How about we just vote Mr. Volikov out of the business?"

"*How about* I tell him how you translate?"

"Or, like you said, we could talk with Farm Supply and see what they can source."

"I will allow you to steal my three shares for his life. Or I will keep my three shares and Maksim will steal your life. And unlike Maksim, I will not back-and-forth barter."

/r/thatescalatedquickly

/r/instant_regret

/r/todayifuckedup

I'm going with TIFU: Today I Fucked Up.

"So be it. Call the lawyers. Let's get this done."

Isaak shakes his head. "They will not come with Bratva in condition they are."

"Which is?"

"Conscious."

"You're kidding."

"Drunk and conscious is problem. See, last lawyer to visit, Bratva force him into transparent drum, lock lid, and roll him into lion's pen. Bratva enjoy this game of being batted around by lion. Screaming lawyer did not. Another time, Konstantin buys old Pershing tank. Big group of Bratva drop lawyer into tank. Of course, lawyer was angry and protesting, but Bratva say drive will only be thirty minutes. *Three days later...* You get the idea. There are many stories like this. Lawyers will not come if Bratva are conscious."

"Can you not just tell them the brothers are sober?"

His answer is a look of withering disdain.

"Asleep, then?"

The look deepens.

"Something?"

"As soon as they hear *that*..." The room fills with the sound of breaking glass, the shout of "I will fuck the entire first row at your funeral," the splinter of wood, and uproarious laughter. "Lawyers will turn at door and leave. We will not get them back for days. Same amount of time it takes for this binge to end. You understand they will drink for days, yes?"

In that case, I suppose it's time to quote Dostoyevsky: *Consciousness is a disease, a real utter disease.*

And I got a bag full of cures.

*   *   *

The only thing not to like about Dostoyevsky is he fervently believed in both God and free will, yet his works are a testament to Fate's guiding hand guaranteeing the most tragic outcome possible. With Dostoyevsky, all small actions lead to one inevitable outcome, one unavoidable disaster, one's inescapable destiny. God's Will, *not* free will. He did not understand the two cannot exist together.

Pushkin, on the other hand, equated divinity with madness. Or was it madness with divinity? Yes, that's it: the visions of the schizophrenic were a blessing from heaven.

Meanwhile, Chekhov and Gorky were analyzing Tolstoy's dream of an infinite desert where his empty shoes were endlessly walking without purpose.

Symbolism was rife in all these artists' works.

Religion, philosophy, symbolism, always the great thinkers of Russian literature were trying to make sense of the senseless.

But Turgenev was such a nihilist he brought the word to Russia and introduced it to the Russian Revolution, saying, "A nihilist is a man who does not bow to any authority, who does not take any principle on trust, no matter how respected the principle is." It's no wonder Demyan has the man inked on his skin, but Demyan is not a nihilist.

Nihilists do not join groups.

There's no worry nihilists (or anarchists) will ever take over the world because, based on their very principles, they cannot work together. Until we're down to just a handful of humans, the world is safe from any demanding concepts such as self-government.

Even so, both the Bratva and the thieves in law would like to call themselves nihilists and anarchists because they don't support the established government, but they govern nonetheless, and you can't be an anarchist unless you follow its rule. Crime and anarchy are no more synonymous than nihilism and existentialism, or fatalism and determinism; so many *isms* there was bound to be a schism.

The break between the thieves in law and the Bratva is also down to the intricacies of philosophy, their style of government, and the application of law. They are very similar yet they remain uniquely different.

Take for instance the definition of family: all thieves are from the same family no matter what Bratva family they serve, while the Bratva hold loyalty only to the family name.

Demyan is a thief, loyal to all thieves, but he's also a brother of the Zomanov Bratva.

Now consider the rule of betrayal: a thief cannot betray a thief, a brother cannot betray a brother, but they can betray each other.

As these two codes collide, the Bratva have it easy but the thieves have it hard. The Bratva only have brothers, but the thieves have in-laws. Family loyalties are stretched for the thieves.

Demyan wants to take over the Zomanov Bratva for the honor of the thieves and in the name of his father. It would become the Zharkov Bratva with Demyan Zharkov as Pakhan.

But for the council of thieves to grant a betrayal against Zomanov, also a thief in law, Konstantin must be stripped of his stars, and then, no longer a thief, Demyan is free to betray the Bratva for the greater good of the thieves.

Terribly, morally complicated this family business is. Not nearly so simple as *Kill the king, wear the crown.*

And in this game, there are a great many wills at play. The will of the thieves, of the Bratva, of the father—God's Will will undoubtedly show its face before it's over—the will of the silovik, the Red State, the government, the will that serves the family, the corporation, its citizens, and the good of the shareholders. In these conflicted associations, I am the only one serving free will, the will of the individual, the will of the anarchist, the free agent, the lone fox, the full moon. I am the only one willing to admit I am acting on selfish grounds, for myself and myself alone. And while it is intellectually honest, I can't really advise it.

There's a reason humans are successful, and it's because we cooperate in groups that benefit society.

If you're going to embrace one of the *isms* (nihilism, anarchism, existentialism, fatalism, determinism), you'll be going it alone, so you damn well better be fully self-reliant.

159

And finding out if you *are* self-reliant while deep in the midst of embracing a few *isms* is nothing short of stupid.

It calls for a sober mind, yet I have no intention of facing this disaster straight.

And I don't think anyone else should either.

We should all be as staggered as the goat still trapped in the lion's pen.

Half the Bratva are already there, and the rest just need a little push.

I dig in my bag of pharmaceuticals for the final shove.

Ambien—as in *Salvadore Dali just painted my skull Ambien*—should do very well.

The Lovers

Of all the misunderstood cards in the deck, the Lovers is second only to Death. Just as Death has nothing to do with mortality, the Lovers have nothing to do with love or sex or marriage or anything remotely sentimental.

The Lovers belong to Gemini, to duality and affiliation, association and combination, and as such, the Lovers represent alchemy, the synergy of substances, say something like vodka and sleeping pills.

While alcohol and benzos are a dangerous combo on your heart, the main cause of death when mixing alcohol and Ambien is driving.

Which means I'll have to hide every one of these lunatics' keys.

Then drug the brothers without dosing any of the principal players required to sign.

Then maybe arrange Volikov's death.

Then get Peter and myself out of Russia.

Then break up with Peter, call off the wedding, and probably go into shameful hiding.

Whoa. Slow down. One thing at a time.

Prepare the Ambien.

Hide the keys.

Don't worry, two things are safe. Everything up and until three is safe. I could even add to that list: drug the Zomanov Bratva.

Prepare the Ambien. Hide the keys. Drug the Zomanov Bratva.

Perfectly safe.

I do realize, of course, the symbolic dangers of preparing the Ambien in the tower, but the actual alchemy will be done in the kitchen where the vodka bottles are stored.

From the Tylenol bottle, I remove all thirty-six Ambien and leave the methaqualone.

On the bedside table, I use the heavy shot glass from earlier to crush the white pills into powder. While each tablet contains only ten milligrams of zolpidem, the inactive ingredients weigh in at nearly half a gram, which makes for a hell of a pile. To ensure it dissolves quickly, I use the side of a credit card to continue chopping until the mound is sufficiently dust-like, then use the card to guide the powder into Demyan's discarded cigarette packet.

Granted, all the grinding is a little like the work of an alchemist... in a tower... but the real magic is when it's added to the vodka. I'm thinking 360 milligrams of active Ambien dissolved in two one-liter bottles of vodka should render all that consume it unconscious, and then Isaak can call the lawyers to come.

But, again, I drive beyond the headlights.

It's time to hide the keys so no one dies either beyond or behind the headlights.

Man, that would be bad. Not the sort of guilt I'd want to live with.

Before leaving the tower, I open my shirt and adjust my bra to lay the Ambien packet flush against my breast, near the heart, where the chakras return to the Tree of Life, at the place represented by the Six of Cups, because, well, you know, a bit of cabalistic safeguarding can't hurt, and why risk being caught skulking around with a packet of white powder?

In the spiral stairs, the echo of my descending footsteps is masked by an angry conversation below.

I recognize Volikov's educated voice. "Do not bore me with the details of how. Your brute methods are of no interest to me. Just get rid of her."

"You *mudojoby*," ballsackfuckers, "have to realize it is not the nineties." Undoubtedly Bratva.

"It is better than the nineties. You are just not clever enough to notice."

"The fuck am I going to do with her?"

"I do not care."

"And how the devil are you going to explain her disappearance?"

"Quiet, someone comes." But the hushed warning is still magnified inside the tower.

"This is three cunts beyond stupid." And the whisper is resonantly clear.

"Go. Quickly. *Now.*"

Rounding the last corner, Volikov stares expectantly up at me, but racing off through the main hall, I think I spot the bare head of what was previously the Polar Bear making for the cover of the conservatory.

Volikov takes my hand and draws me down the last steps, and then, to prevent me from further studying the retreating figure, he positions himself to block the view. He says, "The brothers are about to have a rather medieval dinner outside, to which you are welcome, but if you prefer something less savage, you can dine with me."

His hands are cold. His fingers are thin and graceful, and his touch is so gentle it would not be felt except for the chill. The hands of a water sign.

As the door of the conservatory closes, he releases his grip so his arms drop fluidly back to his sides, and he waits for an answer.

But nothing about the offer is warm, and as I don't particularly want to eat apples with a snake, not with what's happening to Eve in the greenhouse, I say, "Peter is waiting for me." But then, contrary to what is expected, I move for the front door.

Volikov steps in my path to explain, "The quickest way to the backyard is through the *back* of the house. The conservatory, in fact."

"Yes, but I believe I left my sunglasses in the car, which is in front." Along with all the keys.

He rests a hand on my shoulder to stop me going forward. "I will send someone to retrieve them." Then his thumb presses into my muscle and painfully turns me around. "A member of the staff will bring them to you." The long fingers lift from my shoulder to point in the direction he'd like me to leave. "Go have dinner"—and a push with his palm speeds me along—"with Peter."

With Peter, that does sound like an ideal place to be right now.

But I'm only skirting through the conservatory to get to the eastern gallery, then back out front to the cars and the keys.

However, circumnavigating the equatorial jungle is going to prove slow. These lands are in conflict.

Hidden behind the parlor palms is Demyan. "Touch her and die."

Next is the Polar Bear. "I am not a fucking beast. I will ask."

And then Felix. "Like, 'Will you beat your head against my stick?' ask?"

"Who would accept such fuckery? She will not."

"She will not have a choice."

"She will kick you right in the *khren*." Khren = horseradish = dick.

"Who is this contentious she?" I interrupt. "And what are you asking of her?"

The only sound now is the snake retching in the fountain and the soles of my shoes clacking across the tiles.

Demyan emerges from the foliage to grab my arm and spin me to face the stone wall of the house.

In the first shadows of late evening, one shadow jerks and trembles into the eastern gallery, and the other disappears outside.

"Is the she me?"

I don't know if Demyan is puzzling over the truth, or if I said that too fast. Whichever, he's changing topics. "I want you." Then pushing me against the wall, "I cannot wait for night."

His palms slide from my arms over the hourglass of breasts, waist, and hips. He pulls at my clothes to get at my flesh.

His hands are strong and rough, the fingers short, thick, and squared along the tips. The hands of a farmer, a toiler, of

165

manual labor. Hands of purpose. Nothing will slip through his grip. The hands of an Earth sign. The Devil. Capricorn. A goat.

Not at all the sort of thing you'd have inked on your skin in a Russian prison, where the goat is a bitch. Better to go with the bull, Taurus, the Prince of Coins, like Peter.

You can try to disguise one cloven-hoofed ruminant as the other, but there's no mistaking the Devil is Pan, and Pan is a goat. A very randy goat.

And a goat's passion will lead them into all sorts of mischief.

He says, "Here, against the wall. I want to fuck you against the stones."

"We will be caught."

"I know. It will be *azart.*"

With Demyan's mouth on my neck, I glance over his shoulder to see if anyone could be watching. Densely layered foliage conceals us from the backyard, but through the glass panes of the nearby gallery doors I see a trembling shadow stretched long across the interior wall. As the ethereal hand spastically jerks, cigarette ash floats past the glass. I require no psychic third eye to see it's Felix. He's spying.

I try to disentangle, but Demyan's hands are roving under my shirt. I whisper, "Wait a minute," but he growls back, "First, I want to touch your naked flesh."

"Hang on. There is—"

"The silk of your bra."

"—someone in—"

"The skin of your breast."

"—the gallery."

"The heat of—*What is this?*"

166

Dammit.

"What is this?" He pulls the packet from my shirt.

"Don't open it."

He opens it anyway and runs his smallest finger through the contents. "Is this coke?"

"Uh, coke? Yes. *Yes,* it is coke."

He immediately dives in.

Before he can hurt himself, I clamp my hand over his in the packet, and his face questions the over-aggressive action.

Hand still wrapped around his, I step in closer and whisper, "This is for us." With my cheek against his, I murmur, *"For later."* Then taking his lower lip in my mouth, I gently suck, "I promise you," and bite, "we're going to need all of it," and seduce, "for what I'm going to do to you later."

The next bite is hard enough to reclaim the packet and for Demyan to growl, "You excite me."

"You like that?"

"I like."

"Good, because I'm going to excite you in ways you never expected."

"I want to say to hell with *later* and do it now, but first I must do something. Until *later.*" And he presses his face into my neck while breathing long and deep, running his lips across my flesh until he's able to kiss the hollow between my breast. "Until *later* you do us both favor and stay beside Peter. Yes?"

"Peter?"

"Stay with Peter."

With both Volikov and Demyan wanting me at Peter's side, I have to ask, "Why?"

167

He pauses to think, to lie and persuade. "Nothing to worry about. You do this for me. For me"—he puts my hand over his heart—"and for *later*. Yes?"

I need no time to think, to lie or persuade. "Yes, of course. Anything you ask. Find me later."

He waits for me to start crossing the floor for the backyard before moving off for the western gallery. But as soon as I hear the conservatory door close behind him, I spin midstride, intent on returning to the eastern gallery, and plow right into Felix.

The soft-footed sneak-thief is knocked backward. Stumbling sideways, he grabs for me, and I grapple with the flailing limbs and flapping robe, hoping to catch him, but the slick soles of the Armani slippers slide on the tiles.

Everything about his appearance makes him seem like a ward in a nursing home, far too frail to survive the impending fall. My heart actually flutters with fear. I feel it try to jump from my shirt.

His voice pitches high as he clings to my chest. *"Auryea!" Arrghh!*

Leaning back, I try to balance his weight. We spin around. Then next I'm falling. And Felix displays a surprising and quite unexpected strength in stopping it. It's almost startling to be standing still, facing each other.

He smiles. "And they say the *barynya* is dead."

Barynya = Russian folk dance = stamping, kicking, and spinning.

Velvet smoking jacket in disarray, and slippered left foot scrapping along the tiles, he shuffles outside to join his brothers.

*   *   *

Not even in a GTA mod-shop will you see decency flouted like it's flouted in Konstantin's driveway. Never mind the faux marble Maserati or any of the other atrocities from the airport—the pin-striped Bentley lowrider, the metallic gold Land Rover, the stretch six-door Jaguar, or the Unimog draped in camouflage net—because we picked up a few new aberrations at Demyan's sagging mansion. Now we have a Porsche Spyder with a three-tiered chrome exhaust the size of a British Mini, and also a Cadillac with white walls, curb feelers, and two-foot mermaid hood ornament; there's an A8 with a flame painted cowl induction hood, and even a Mercedes S with Fendi embossed leather fender flares, but the coup de grâce on modesty is the 50's Studebaker with smoky glass T-tops and rear spoiler.

The Russian word for shame is pozor. Don't worry, the nouveau riche in the backyard aren't familiar with the word either.

So secure they are in their wealth and numbers, they've left the keys to their kingdoms unguarded. And I'm going to hide them.

Starting at the iron gates and looping around the circle drive, I remove keys from ignitions, center consoles, sun visors, and cup holders. I find them on the floorboards, under the seats, and beside the grenade launcher. Stretching into the Bentley, I take the keys clipped to the rosary around the rearview mirror, then crawl into the Land Rover to find the keys beside the weapons crate with the RPG. Finally, I scale the four-foot tires of the Unimog to scramble into the cab.

The minimalist interior doesn't offer many places to look, and the keys are in none of them.

169

Possibly problematic, but there's really no time to dwell on it.

Back in the castle, I figure the safest place for the keys is in the living room, in the monstrous cabinet in the corner, the one with six drawers and a dozen locked doors, the cupboard you find in almost every Russian household, the hulking heirloom you never see anyone use, not at any time, not ever. It exists solely to loom and bequeath.

Being raised in an orphanage, Konstantin starts this particular legacy, and he's chosen to encumber future Zomanov generations with a heavily carved and gilded Louis XIV replica.

Dumping nine sets of keys into the lowest drawer, I notice a stack of playing cards.

Russian cards.

I can't resist.

Scooping them up, the deck feels light, but that's expected. Centuries ago Russia dispensed with one through five, so the deck holds only thirty-six cards. Six to ten and four in the court: the Ace, the King, the Dame, and Valet.

The cards are old. Older than anything in the house. And they've been used and used again, shuffled and dealt until the paper is soft, the original satin finish nothing more than a detail known to collectors.

I want to see what fortune they reveal, but the tattered edges would make an overhand shuffle rough. And a riffle would be sacrilege.

Instead, I hold the deck in my left hand and let the fingers of my right gently displace the weight of cards, from the bottom to the top, feeling for the place the deck wants to cut. They all want to break somewhere. They all have something to say.

Cards like this carry history. They're infused with the places they've been, the events they've been through. It affects them. Some decks become too optimistic, some only tell the worst kinds of truth, but none of them lie. They can't lie. They can only show the future and the past as their handlers experience it.

That's why serious diviners always have a deck that no one touches except themselves. I have three: one for friends, one for family, and one held only by me.

The cards from Konstantin's cabinet feel like they've been through the hands of many. I'm guessing a memento from prison.

After testing the weight of the cards three times, I let the deck split where it wants. Turning the stack in my right hand, I look at the bottom card.

The ten of swords, Ruin.

Definitely prison. Coming from or going to is about the only question.

Another question might be: Is this Konstantin's past or my future?

And also: As the card is ruled by the Sun (Leo/Konstantin) in Gemini (me), could it be our fates are twined?

And maybe: Would imprisonment include—

"You know why farmer always kills fox?"

Alyona. Turning around, she's in the archway to the living room with the right corner of her mouth slightly higher than the left.

"Fox can never take just enough. You ever see chicken house after fox comes?"

"Actually, no."

"Chicken house is nothing but feathers and shit. Feathers and shit everywhere."

"Thank you for the image."

"Fox sees opportunity and loses mind. Fox cannot stop killing. Fox will spend all night burying bodies. More than fox can ever eat. Why? Because fox always goes too far."

"Is that from Aesop's?"

"Konstantin thinks you could be fox."

"And I think Demyan is the Devil and you're the Queen of Swords, but we won't know for certain till it's over."

The left side of her mouth rises to meet the right. She's flattered. And who wouldn't be with a title like Queen of Swords?

Before making the deck whole again, I look once more at the ten of swords. Ruin *is* part of this queen's arsenal.

Behind her in the foyer, nearly a dozen women in heels clack across the polished marble for the stairs. Alyona throws an offhanded gesture toward the bedrooms on the second and third levels, and says, "We dress for dinner. Maybe you stop breaking into chicken house and join us?"

"Wait a second."

With only Alyona in sight, and only Alyona in mind, I run my fingers over the edge of the cards again, displacing the weight, and letting the deck break where it will.

I don't even have to look to know it's Ruin. But I do. And it is.

The decks all have something to say, and if you're listening correctly, they say it over and over. The only thing that will stop them repeating themselves is to pack them in salt. But as these cards aren't mine to wipe clean, I replace them in the lowest drawer with the keys while casually mentioning to the queen, "So, *umm,* listen... maybe don't drink the vodka."

Turning around, I notice her eyes have widened in alarm.

Racing to Ruin or avoiding it, I'm no longer certain what I'm doing, but it still seems responsible to add, "And maybe don't let your girlfriends up there drink it either."

When the queen's brows rise with unspoken questions, I say, "Don't make a big deal of it," which leaves her lips to twist in disbelief.

While her posture demands answers I can't possibly give, it seems prudent to offer, "I'll transfer another Bitcoin, shall I?"

"Make it two."

*   *   *

The armorer from the never-ending Renaissance fair that was my childhood taught me more than just Russian. He also showed me how to produce steel by combining carbon with iron. The fair's potter taught me to make porcelain by adding bone to clay. And one of the acrobats had me make a speedball by chopping heroin into coke. Combining Ambien and alcohol also results in something unique. It's called a Sleep Stalker.

173

It sounds a little creepy, but such is the outcome: people *will* get weird.

It's been nearly a year since I last went sleep stalking, and slinking through an unknown kitchen stirs a distant memory of looking for a hair dryer, of wet braids, and an electric whisk...

Best not to dwell on it.

In Konstantin's kitchen, a member of staff washes dishes and another grinds meat, and neither takes notice of me slipping into the storage room where the vodka is stored.

Taking two bottles from an open case, I set them on a shelf, remove their caps, and then reach into my shirt for the Ambien.

It is not over my heart chakra.

Or under my heart chakra.

Or anywhere near the Tree of Life.

As my hands roam over my body with a desperation greater than Demyan's, I ignore the angry slam of the kitchen door, the aggravated entry of someone stamping across the granite floor, the whisk of steel, and the clash of pottery, but there's no way to miss the enraged explanation: "As if throwing a damn table in the pool is not enough, Konstantin is fucking a whore in the sauna, and goddamn Felix has taken both my marble pastry board and knife to cut out lines of coke."

Felix...

Lines of coke...

Oh. Dear. God. Please let the flutter of my heart have been fear and not a pickpocket with Parkinson's.

Death

There's Ambien-in-alcohol weird and then there's Ambien-mistaken-for-cocaine weird. The first seeps pleasantly into your blood, while the other rips across your neurons like synaptic Pop Rocks.

Hurrying from the kitchen, down the eastern gallery, and through the conservatory, I've only just stepped foot on the grass, but it's obvious I'm too late to do anything but watch.

On the picnic table is the marble pastry board, the chef's knife, and what looks like eighteen one-gram lines of coke. There's also Demyan's crumpled cigarette packet, which most recently contained thirty-six crushed Ambiens.

One of the assembled Bratva has just chopped out lines of pharmaceutical-grade magic realism, and they all plan to rail it. Right up the nose and directly to the brain, a bullet train of surreal.

Crowding around the table, eighteen heads drop in quick succession to the board.

"It burns."

"I do not think this is snow."

"Horse?"

Vicious comes up snarling from the experience, "Fuck no. Horse does not kick like that."

"Peter, what the fuck is it?"

"Give him the straw."

"Do a line, man."

"Fuck. Me. On. Fire. What is this shit?"

"Peter snorts it, so is not poison."

"But what is it?"

"Stand aside. I will tell you. ... *Fuck your mother. Burn.*"

"Do you feel it?"

"I do not feel anything."

"Maybe that is good."

"Maybe it is."

"Is good?"

"Is something."

"Stop whispering."

"No one whispers."

"Stop."

"Whoa."

"This is the most I have ever been."

"Huh?"

"I am surrounded by distance."

"What?"

"The lag is bad."

"Speak up."

"I have over five hundred ping right now. *Fuck*, I will be kicked from EU server."

"Those European *pedophile bitch* motherfuckers. I fucking hate Euro *cocksucker* on EU servers."

"I think I'm starting to understand Russian."

"Did you hear that? I must be on US server. **Oh shit, boi, waddup!**"

176

"Yeah, I'm starting to understand—"

"Mid or feed. Pick up gem. Farming Divine. This is all the English I know."

"—but it sounds like DOTA."

"Is fucking *GG* for us. Pink is *noob*."

"Is this a game? Are we in a game?"

"My graphics are pixeled. My ping is shit. My rig is overheating. Restart."

"Did you fucking yodel? You know I fucking hate yodeling."

"I'm starting to think more like I did when it began than I do now."

"Turn it on and off. Turn it on and off! *Turn it on and off!*"

"You motherfucker, you know I hate yodeling." **The Strongman turns the screaming Elvis off with a punch to the face.**

In the long silence that follows, the brothers stare down at him until James Dean finally asks, "How do we turn him back on?"

"Put him in pool."

"He *was* running hot."

"Pick him up."

"He is fucking heavy."

"Everyone, pick him up."

"Hurry, he is hot."

"Get him in pool."

Johnny Rotten, Sid Vicious, Louis Vuitton, Felix, the Fat Man, the Ken Doll, the Mongolian with a Mohawk, and one of six tattooed men splash into the pool carrying Elvis.

"Put him on table."

"Take his feet."

"Get his head out of water."

"Hold table still."

"You will drown him."

"Table is rocking."

"Ocean is rough today."

"Take his head."

"No, asshole, that is foot."

"Fucking waves."

"Roll him back over."

"Not that way."

"For fuck sake!"

"You think you know better way to do this more stupid?"

That gives them all pause.

Holding Elvis's head, Louis Vuitton eventually breaks the spell by asking, "What does it mean if your dick burns when you piss?"

"No idea. The water is keeping mine cool."

"You lose most of body heat from your head."

"Of your dick?"

"No, of your head."

"He has a lot of hair on his head."

178

"Could be why he is overheating."

"If we are going to save him, it has to come off."

"For the love of god, someone get a razor."

And that, for the uninitiated, is Ambien. That's how you wake up in a pool on a picnic table shaved completely naked.

*　　*　　*

It wouldn't be such an unmitigated disaster if it stopped there. But it won't. Not tonight. Not when seventeen brothers are still awake.

Already, the Mongolian with a Mohawk is peeling off from the group for the lion's pen, and Vicious is standing on a chair over the grill using a 9-iron to knock coals into the woods.

When Demyan exits the conservatory to stand beside me and stare, Peter is on his hands and knees, his face two inches from the turf. Nearby, still dripping wet from the pool, Louis Vuitton seems to be stuck in the crane pose, Rotten is trying to fit his knee in his mouth, and Felix is talking to Konstantin, but Konstantin is nowhere to be seen.

In that unique tone produced when confusion mixes with disbelief and results in anger, Demyan asks, "Kakóvo čórta?" What kind of demon?

You think I'm going to tell the Devil which demon broke loose from hell? Not on my life. No, I'm going to shrug and act clueless.

"*Yo*—what-the-fuck?—*stop it.*" Demyan goes after the Ken Doll who is slicing the air with the hunting knife from earlier, swearing, "Fucking webs everywhere."

179

It's a good moment to take control of Peter.

"Okay, sweetie, party's over. Let's go. You did good. Mission: success. But it's time to leave now. Come on. Upsy-daisy." I repeatedly try to haul him from the ground, but he's utterly absorbed and determined to stay down.

"How have I missed this for so long?"

"Come on, Peter."

"It's so obvious."

"Get up."

"It's amazing."

"Let's go."

"Did you know this?"

"What's that?" Hooking under his arm, I strain to lift him.

"Grass is... *alive.*"

"Yeah, sweetie, grade school biology there."

"It's breathing."

"Respiring."

"Totally. You know what else repeat inspires?"

"Tell me while we walk."

"Oh my god, baby, we can't walk on it. It's *alive.*"

"It doesn't mind."

"Don't. Walk. On. Grass. The signs were everywhere. *Eek!*" He looks down in horror, raises his right foot, then his left, then his right, and continues to swap feet until he's a caricature of Yosemite Sam.

Grabbing him by the face, I ask, "Did you know there's a storm on Jupiter that's more than three hundred years old and

180

twice the size of Earth? Did you know if you had a dollar for every year the universe existed, you still wouldn't be one of the fifty richest people? If God scattered humanity across the world for building the Tower of Babel, what's he going to do over the International Space Station? Did you know Adam strangled Eve in the Garden of Eden with the Snake? I didn't either. Do you want to see it? Come on, then, I'll show you." (No one who's worked the Renaissance circuit for more than a year hasn't dealt with a day tripper skitzing on psychedelics sold to them by the magicians. You quickly learn to recontextualize.)

With his attention now galaxies away from the grass, Peter follows me into the conservatory in an awe-inspired daze.

As promised, I lead him to Adam and Eve.

The fountain gurgles and groans and the struggle sounds so real I wonder if I took Ambien as well. Then, from the bulk of twisted limbs, the Polar Bear lurches into view with Alyona in a choke hold.

"Fucking fantastic," Peter exclaims. "Three-D art is totally future-proof."

The Polar Bear startles to see us, and Alyona uses the moment to drop forward and sideways and punch him in the groin.

Peter winces.

In a twist that takes her to the ground, she slips from his hold, grabs the closest terracotta pot (the one with a peace lily), and swings up to break it across his face.

Still wincing, Peter says, "Owwie wah-wah."

The lily and a shower of loose soil fall to the ground between them. Across the Polar Bear's face, where the impact broke skin, dirt mingles with blood, and a shard of orange pottery penetrates his cheek.

The Polar Bear strikes out with his fists, but still insists, "I am not trying to kill you," to which Alyona retorts, "I am not trying either."

She takes what remains of the pot and dashes it against his temple.

The Polar Bear staggers. While he's defenseless, Alyona couples her hands into a double fist and batter-up strikes. His knees drop to the floor and his head follows.

I mutter, "My god," and Peter asks, "Why hath thou forsaken him?"

With the Polar Bear's hair wound between her fingers, Alyona smashes his head into the edge of the fountain.

Peter intones, "Now she lays him down to sleep."

Alyona keeps bashing. Smashing and repeatedly bashing until blood spreads through the water.

And Peter keeps rhyming, "She prays the Lord his soul to keep."

When the snake begins to spew a stream of pink vomit across Adam's feet, Alyona holds the Polar Bear's head under water until he bubbles like Eve.

Then Peter concludes, "If he should die before he wakes," *gur-blurble-blurble,* "she prays the Lord his soul to take."

Turning to me, Peter says, "That prayer always scared the bejesus out me as a child."

* * *

* * *

When you're sleep stalking on Ambien and alcohol, nothing seems real, and the moment your attention strays from something it ceases to exist. *Poof.* Gone. Pretty much gone forever. Oh sure, you might feel a disturbing sense of déjà vu when a sober scene unfolds too similar to an Ambien scene, but as there's no chance in hell Peter is ever going to witness a scene like that again, we can effectively say Alyona never killed the Polar Bear because Peter will never be troubled by the memory of it.

Lucky fucking Peter.

Gazing up at the Bermuda palms, he has no recollection what happened twenty seconds ago, or that Adam's feet are still being splattered in pink pools of snake spit.

Alyona unwinds her fingers from the Polar Bear's hair and tells me, "He tried to kill me."

I nod with emphatic agreement because she is not someone I am going to argue the small details with.

She says, "Konstantin will kill me."

I nod to that too.

She says, "You have to help me."

And I nod to that as well because the little fox is not about to say *No* to the Queen of Swords after what she just did to a polar bear.

With his attention now on the glass ceiling, Peter asks, "Do you honestly think that can hold the weight of the ocean?"

Alyona looks at the ceiling, then at Peter, then at the dead man in the fountain.

Peter asks me, "How did we get here?"

183

"We were driven."

"In a boat?"

"No, a car."

"Where do you think we are?"

"Bereznik."

"No, baby, this is BioShock. This is Rapture. We're *Twenty Thousand Leagues Under the Sea*."

Alyona pulls the Polar Bear's head from the water and says, "We put him in car and drive to woods."

But Peter is resolute. "I'm not going anywhere without a diving suit."

"For good of God," Alyona snaps, "exactly how drunk are you?"

"On a scale of one to Russian, I'm Vladimir Putin."

While Alyona considers finding another peace lily, Peter two-step hip-hops to an impromptu song. "Vlad, Vlad, Vladimir Putin. Soon to be puking. You ain't been drunk till you've seen Rasputin. Wooting, tooting, Vladimir Putin."

Ignoring Peter's continuing performance, I ask Alyona, "Why was he trying to kill you?"

"Is plan of Maksim Volikov. He protects Peter against Konstantin who uses me for kompromat. Understand?"

Not only do I understand both Volikov and Konstantin—not to mention Demyan—have plans to blackmail Peter for control of the timber empire, I also understand the Polar Bear was working for Volikov but sharing his plans with Demyan and Felix, which makes him something of a double agent and further indicates Demyan and Felix are allies, but mostly I understand we can't stand here with a body until we're caught.

"Peter, sweetie." I step into his dance and get twirled around. "One of our new friends clonked his head on the fountain and needs a little help getting to the car and hospital. Do you think you could help carry him?"

"Help? Baby, I am the tank that carries the team."

"Excellent. Follow me. He's right over here by the—"

"Jesus! Is that blood? Someone needs to tone down the splatter effects. Hoss, you okay?" Peter kneels down to pat the Polar Bear's shoulder.

"He's unconscious. You'll have to carry him. Maybe use the fireman's lift."

"Good idea, because I smell smoke. And where there's smoke, there's fire. And I fight fires. I am Morris and Hugo's captain of the fire department. Chief firefighter, that's me, fighting fires in every major account."

"Devil take me," Alyona explodes. "Carry to car!"

"Extrapediately, boss. Just tell me where you want him."

The Porsche Spyder is nearest the gate, but have you seen the storage space? Not really suitable for transporting bodies. There is one car, however, that could carry all four thieves in law (including the fat one) and still have room in the trunk for a case of vodka and grenade launcher. And from where it's parked, it could cut straight across the circle drive and be on the road in a flash. Plus, given a choice, what would any true, decent, and patriotic American move the body of a dead Russian gangster in?

I tell Alyona, "You direct Peter. I'll get the keys and meet you at the Studebaker."

*   *   *

185

*　　*　　*

The car is from the 50s, the T-tops from the 80s, and the scene from anywhere but Russia: two men in the backseat, a woman behind the wheel, and another closing the door to ride shotgun. The Polar Bear's wet head rests against Peter's shoulder. It could almost be mistaken for affection, if not for the watercolor hue of red seeping across Peter's shirt.

Giving Alyona the keys, I have to ask, "Don't you think the trunk would have been a more appropriate place to put him?"

"Need keys for trunk. Now we need keys for escape."

While she starts the car, Peter says, "Key figures will reach escape velocity before stick figures."

And Alyona asks, "Did he drink vodka you warn me not to drink?"

As she drops the column shift into reverse, I mutter, "Uh... sort of."

"And did *he*"—she points a polished fingernail across the Bakelite steering wheel to Johnny Rotten in mid-Limbo with a tendril of smoke—"also *sort of* drink vodka?"

"He might have had a sip."

Wrestling the wheel fully to the left to reverse, then three-sixty back to drive, she glances at the dead man in the rearview and concedes, "Maybe now is not time to judge."

"If we're lucky, we'll both have time for that later."

And good thing for us, luck and time are intrinsically linked. Fate would have it that the timing of your birth determines your measure of luck. You're either born lucky or you're not, though the only way to know for sure is to test it.

186

The problem with that is most people find out they're not lucky at the worst possible moment, usually in the throes of death or arrest.

I know I am lucky and that Peter is lucky. The Polar Bear we might assume is not lucky, and Alyona is still a mystery. Best case scenario, the ratio of luck in the car is on our side, and at worst we're traveling fifty-fifty until we dump the body. We are four bodies traveling on four wheels in an eight-cylinder car in the eighth hour of night.

These details matter.

Four and eight are in motion.

Four and eight are in play.

Four is stability, but eight is trouble.

When we dump the body, we'll be three and it will probably be nine, and three and nine are lucky. Lucky like nothing else. Three will keep us safe and nine ensures success.

It's all down to the power of three: the Rule of Three, the Three Ways, the Holy Trinity, the Law of Return, the universe's triadic nature as found in the Tao Te Ching, the Bhagavad-Gita, the Tibetan Book of the Dead, the Bible, and Kabbalah.

One is the essence of God, but three is God manifest.

Three times three is nine.

Three is the idea. Nine is the realization.

Three is the plan and nine its fulfillment.

Three is the start, but nine is completion.

Three is God, and nine will save your ass.

I don't really believe any of this, but as we leave behind Konstantin's modern castle to enter the surrounding woods, I'm completely counting on it.

187

Four miles of access road leads to the T-junction of a dirt road that runs south to the small town of Bereznik and north to the sawmill. Alyona turns north.

The road grows thinner. The trees denser. The summer sun is blocked. Darkness envelopes, and something is off. More off than just driving through the woods with a dead man.

Strange shades pulse in the woods.

The light is eerie.

Hues of yellow, blue, and red surround us.

Alyona stares into the trees and asks, "Xúli?" What the fuck?

"Military radiation," Peter whimpers. "Medical experiments. Alien abduction. Sasquatch."

Foot on the brake, Alyona slowly brings the car to a halt. The woods radiate in shades of yellow, green, blue, purple, red, and orange.

"We shouldn't stop here," Peter says. "Never stop under the mothership."

"Xúli?" Alyona repeats.

The woods pulse yellow, green, blue, purple, red, and orange.

"I don't like this," I whisper.

Alyona takes her foot off the brake, and the car creeps forward.

The light follows.

On either side of the road, against the trunks of the trees, it shines: yellow, green, blue, purple, red, and orange.

Alyona speeds up.

The light does too.

Alyona slams on the brakes.

I scream as the Polar Bear's face slams against the back of the seats and the light from the woods illuminates the forward splatter in pale shades of yellow, green, blue, purple, red, and orange.

Alyona stomps on the gas. The Polar Bear shoots back against Peter, Peter screams louder, and the light keeps pace.

Ruts in the road slam the undercarriage into the hard surface, and the light in the woods climbs the trees. The leaves glow yellow, then green, then blue, then purple, then red, then orange.

Turning delirious with fear, Peter shrieks, "Trix are for kids!"

Alyona goes faster.

The light flickers with the speed, jumps with the potholes, dives with the impact, but always stays right outside the windows.

Yellow, green, blue, purple, red, and orange.

Alyona says, "Devil."

Skidding to a stop, she says, "No more."

She says, "Peter, find out what is."

And Peter sneers, "Oh sure."

He hugs the Polar Bear to his side and says, "You play with snakes, and then when dad gets mad, you want me to handle it."

He says, "You go explain it to him."

Alyona turns to screech over the bench seats, *"Find out what is!"*

"You're not my mom!"

189

But he still does what she says. Gently opening the door, he peeks over the running boards. He slides along the seat, leaning down to the road, stretching to see beneath the car, and he squeals. He squeals high and wild and beats the back of the seat while screeching, "Go! Go! Go!"

And in sympathetic terror, Alyona stamps on the gas.

The Studebaker shoots forward, then careens sideways.

Inside the vast interior, four bodies are thrown to the left.

Peter screams.

The light follows.

The four tires slide.

The four bodies are hurled back right.

I scream.

The light pulses.

The Studebaker spins broadside, and the light leaves the woods to illuminate the road.

As the car fishtails, Peter warbles, "It's beneath us!" and Alyona hand-over-hand spins the steering wheel right, then left, then right again.

When the car finally lurches straight again, Alyona sighs and mutters, *"Ux."* Oof.

Resting back against the upholstery, she shakes her head in dismay and allows the weight of 1950's steel to slow the car to a roll.

Flexing her shoulders, she straightens her back before asking me, "Is contagious, yes?"

The woods still pulse yellow, green, blue, purple, red, and orange.

190

Peter mewls a sound of fear, and I ask with dread, "Is it?"

"It is," she confirms.

"Oh god, is it lethal? Can it kill us? Is there a cure? Jesus Christ, what is it?"

"Yes, yes, and no. Is American overreaction."

*   *   *

Engine idling, we stand in the road in the Bereznik forest, surrounded by unnatural lights, staring at the horror that is the Studebaker.

Not only does the 50's classic have smoky glass T-tops and rear spoiler, it also sports a pulsing undercarriage lit in all the vibrant colors of a carnival ride.

Yellow, green, blue, purple, red, and orange, it pulses.

Yellow, green, blue, purple, red, and orange, it lights up the woods.

Yellow, green, blue, purple, red, and orange, it is as far from discreet as the Sun from Neptune.

Three hours above the horizon, the nearest star struggles to compete. It casts a fire-like glow over the western forest, and spread out before it is what looks like fog but smells like smoke.

Alyona says, "Is direction of sawmill."

Peter—with no memory older than twenty seconds—is bent at the waist, hands swirling through the lights at the side of the car, whispering to himself, "Nothing can prepare you for the Aurora Borealis. I wonder what it tastes like," and he drops to his knees.

191

For the sake of decency, Alyona and I look away.

Alyona asks, "What was in vodka?"

"Probably best not to say."

"You think that"—she throws a hand in the direction of Peter—"is bigger secret than that." She points at the Polar Bear.

I look to the smoke spreading in the west and say, "We won't know until it's over, but it certainly has the potential."

"You start fire?"

"Depends on how you attribute blame. Indirectly, perhaps, but more directly it was one of the brothers teeing hot coals off the barbecue pit."

She nods, mostly to acknowledge the oddness of it, and then says, "Drunk or sober, brothers are always trouble."

"And the trouble in the back seat? What are we doing with it?"

"Let us drive one trouble to another and see what it offers."

*　*　*

My plans, Peter's future, Morris & Hugo's investment, Demyan and Volikov's schemes, Konstantin's fortune, and the Bereznik forest are all on fire.

This is exactly the kind of shit you can expect from the Tower.

Same goes for the dead man in the back seat.

The sooner we're rid of him the sooner some measure of luck might return.

192

Alyona is driving toward the fire. Undercarriage throwing out lurid colors, we're a beacon in the woods, a carnival ride gone AWOL, an honest-to-god spectacle of Gravitron proportions, and none of the after-factory buttons on the dash will stop it.

The shiny silver switch beside the radio looks promising, but flicking it only results in a thudding bass, sans music.

Peter says, "My heart is pounding."

The big dial near defrost has a certain appeal, but twisting it does nothing.

Peter says, "Bummer."

On the column is a chrome wand, but on shifting it the instrument panel flips to digital.

Peter says, "My ass is hot."

Mine is too.

I'm starting to suspect the bummer dial was seat heating.

Twisting a knob beside the switch sends Russian rockabilly blaring through the tree tops.

Peter says, "No to that shit."

Still untried are the buttons in the roof, the mixer slides on the armrest, and the lever on the floor.

I stare at the buttons with skepticism.

"Why not push it?" Alyona asks. "Afraid it will give us away?"

The Russian accent is so naturally sardonic, I don't know if she's serious when she says, "I think you should push it."

"Really?"

"Abso*lutely.*"

"Something has to turn the lights off. Peter likes to say that, statistically speaking, every failure brings a person closer to success."

"You know what I hear Peter say? Bridges exist to cross or burn."

Stopped at a fork in the road, Alyona considers the possibilities. To the left, the trees are young and spindly thin, and to the right, straddling the river, is the Soviet era sawmill that Morris & Hugo plan to refurbish. On all sides of the mill, the ground is worked bare and littered with the unprofitable refuse of the mill: mountains of bark and dust, heaps of side slabs and splintered boards, all the free waste that ensures Morris & Hugo's future paper mill will be profitable. The bulk of the yard—the drying sheds and round logs—is on the opposite side of the river across a rusted steel bridge.

Peter leans into the front seat to say, "Cross it or burn it but never ignore it."

As smoke rolls from the western forest and seeps into the new growth of unplanned pines nearer the mill, I warn Alyona, "This may not be the moment to literally apply corporate metaphors."

"It's the *Art of War*, baby, and I'm your general. Drive this tank to the frontline so I can slap them with my saber."

"I do not think that is Sun Tzu," Alyona says, "but we will cross bridge."

"I always suggest crossing over burning. Every time you cross a bridge, you create the opportunity for a new relationship. New relationships are the life force of—*Jesus*

194

Christl!" Peter's eyes finally see what lies beyond the hood. "What the hell are you doing?"

"I am crossing bridge."

"Why?" he shrieks "Why would you drive into *that?"*

"Because there is fire."

"Then pray for forgiveness and turn-the-fuck-around!"

"Steel bridge will not burn. We must cross." She's neither an idiot nor following Peter's advice, she's smirking. She's playing with language and fate. She's the Queen of Swords from the court of air, and Peter's earthly concerns don't trouble her.

Another time under different circumstances and without the Ambien, Peter wouldn't stand for this. At the moment, though, he doesn't have a lot of sway because he can't remember there's anything worth swaying. A steel strut catches his attention, and he follows it along the side windows, past the Polar Bear's head, and then he's saying, "Pretty river. Can we go swimming, Mom?"

He's not that far off. Alyona reminds me of his mother as well. Both scary as hell, but also, if you remember, his mother is represented by the card Justice. You might know her as Lady Justice. You know, the righteous woman with the sword? Kind of like...

"We will stop at sawmill. Peter, you will take our friend and put him at top of—" She turns left off the bridge and points to the massive mound of discarded wood. *"—pile,"* she decides to call it.

The accent is so strong, Peter repeats, "Pie-el?"

"Pyre," I correct.

"Pie-err?" she asks.

"Pierre?" Peter taps the Polar Bear's cheek.

"If I understand your plan, it's a pyre."

"Ah, yes, funeral pyre." She smiles with appreciation. "I like this word. It rhymes with fire, no?"

"As it happens, yes."

"Is good plan, no?"

The pile she stops beside is fifteen feet tall at its peak, thirty feet wide at its base, and it runs the length of the mill, so about eighty feet long. There's a few more by the drying sheds and another along the river. The rounded edges of the trees that can't be cut into symmetrical lumber lie jumbled and splintered crossway and diagonal across each other. With air moving freely through the lattice of scrap, it's a perfect bonfire that will burn for days.

"It's a good plan."

Alyona points to me and says, "Fire." Then pointing to herself she says, "Pyre. Fire Pyre." And she laughs.

"Don't"—I shake my head—"name us."

"*Awww,*" she mocks. "You want Bitcoin back?"

I look at her from the top of my eyes.

"You don't get Bitcoin back," she says. "You buy friend. You have friend. Now come, friend, we put fire to pyre."

*   *   *

"I don't know, baby, this doesn't seem right."

Peter isn't really buying my story that the Polar Bear is a dead king, we his acolytes, and the pyre his royal death right.

196

The day trippers at the Renaissance fair would have devoured it, but that's not really Peter's scene. I need to think corporate.

"We're downsizing, sweetie. No, we're restructuring. We're shooting puppies. That's it: we're shooting puppies."

"Man, I *hate* to be the one to shoot the puppy."

"Nobody likes it, but we're doing the needful."

"Better gist me on the mission then."

"The criticality of it cannot be understated. If we don't de-integrate that liability from our corporate memory, Morris and Hugo will have to defer success, and you'll be totally hosed."

"Christ, baby, you should have disambiguated this sooner. Have we got strats on the situation?"

"You need to left lane the liability to the top of the solution."

"The doability of that I can fully operationalize."

While Peter hefts the liability from the back seat of the Studebaker and drags him to the base of the de-integration solution, Alyona says, "If you keep talking like that, I will start shooting babies."

"Ah, but here's the crux," I tell her. "It only works with puppies because everyone loves puppies."

"You don't love babies?"

"You don't love puppies?"

"I like cats."

"Yes, of the choices, they are most preferable."

"Babies just grow up to be people, and people are assholes," Peter says. He has the Polar Bear's arms over his shoulders and is slow walking him up the slope of a plank. Where it intersects with another splice of long wood, he throws the body over, then climbs in front and drags him farther up the pile.

"Cats can be assholes too," Alyona says, "but in respectable way."

"I always wanted a couple of otters," Peter calls down. He hefts the Polar Bear over another slab and then crawls over his stomach to take him by the hands again. "I wanted to live by the river and feed them fish—fish I'd trapped in the river with baskets—and give them toys I'd carved from wood." He pulls the Polar Bear higher, saying, "I dreamed of building a log cabin, felling trees, hunting deer, cooking over an open fire, living life like a real mountain man." Near the top of the pile, he stands up and looks east, past the sawmill and into the field of sawn trunks. "Like this. Look at this rugged beauty. This is raw nature at its finest." He takes it in with a deep breath. "I've never seen anything more stunning."

Whatever the Ambien is seeing in the east, it's not nearly as wondrous as what waits in the west.

Eyes drifting slowly past the bridge, the full panorama comes into view and Peter's mouth falls open. He shudders. He sways. He hurtles down the pyre in ten leaps and runs past us for the car, explaining, "Solar annihilation!"

Scrambling into the back seat, he slams the door, then knocks on the glass as though he doesn't already have our attention. He shouts, "I know how it ends! We have to find a scientist!"

Casually, Alyona opens the driver's door to sit crooked behind the wheel. With her feet outside on the ground, she turns the ignition switch just enough to power the undercarriage lights and the cigarette lighter, and then she lies across the seat to rummage in the glove box for paper.

Peter looks over his shoulder and says with despair, "We should have teched."

Tossing a booklet over the seats, Alyona tells him, "Find exit strategy, Peter."

As Peter rips through the pages in a panic, I notice the smoke in the west has been consumed by flames. A cloud of billowing orange travels the treetops, eating up foliage and limbs. With much of the woods now crackling and hissing, and the roar of acceleration growing louder, Peter's terror is duly warranted.

I look back to the sawmill in the fire's path.

It's not going to be a great loss.

Well, I mean, it's definitely going to burn to the ground, but the building itself is so impoverished and antiquated, no one should shed any tears. Open to the river on each end, it's a throwback to an era when mills floated logs for transport. It's an environmentalist's nightmare. A radical one would happily come and strike the match themselves. But we don't have a match, so Alyona is putting the red coils of the cigarette lighter to a bundle of official looking paperwork.

Peter's twenty second memory is no longer looking for an exit strategy but is instead obsessed with smoothing out the pages of the booklet. Because his hands are working about two inches above the page, he'll be busy until the Ambien starts to wonder what the words taste like.

The flames have now reached the edge of new growth. Driven by the wind and drawn by the river, the first waves of heat roll across the mill's yard, and at this point, setting the pyre alight is just a gratuitous precaution, but one Alyona isn't going to ignore. She puts the torch of paperwork to the slivers and shavings at the base of the pile, and lets the draft from the forest fan the flames.

Above, the Polar Bear lies crooked and hapless like all the other debris in the heap. One leg crosses a slab of heart wood, the other a shattered half round, then an arm is thrown over his head against a shattered beam. In the backseat against Peter's chest, it was easy to believe the lie told to Peter—that he was just a careless drunk, a hapless souse, a simple lush who'd bonked his noggin—but on top the scrap pile, he is unmistakably dead.

With little sympathy, Alyona offers as a memorial, "Not best fighter, but loyal. Dust to dust, ash to ash"—she shrugs—"return, yes?"

"Yeah, definitely. We should get back."

Tower

I've not even consumed any Ambien but reality still seems off. Off because odd is normalizing. Konstantin's dacha doesn't look nearly as garish as before, and the Studebaker is even less obscene beside it. Then James Dean, clipping across the front yard in a bikini bottom and leather jacket, doesn't illicit even a sideways glance from Alyona.

As she leads the way to the front door, he trots past us for the front gate, repeating, "Nyem, nyem, nyem, nyem, nyem."

Nyem is to nyet what nope is to no.

And whatever is going on in the backyard, Dean is nyeming right the hell out of it.

What should concern us, but doesn't, not appreciably, is the sound of fireworks, or maybe gunfire, or possibly just backfire. I'd like to think backfire for no other reason than the Unimog is gone.

The only keys I couldn't find to hide, someone must have had on them. Who they are, where they've gone, and what they've done getting there, these are details I could easily live the rest of my life without knowing.

Just like I don't really want to know why the Blond with Cornrows is dropping from a second-floor window, or what the Mongolian with a Mohawk is doing under the Land Rover with a lighter.

Opening the door, Alyona doesn't slow to ask, "Want to tell me what was in vodka?"

"Not really." After accessory to murder, I don't really want to anything.

In the foyer, we step over a tattooed man wrapped up tight and sleeping in the tapestry—ripped straight from the wall—of Saint John's Ascension.

Alyona points to Peter and tells me, "Change shirt," and then pointing to her own blood covered attire, says, "I change too."

But any thought of ascending the stairs to the bedrooms is abandoned when we hear the angry shout, "I will punch you with my dick!" and watch a military-grade smoke canister bounce end-over-end down the hall.

Nyem.

"While that resolves itself," I tell Alyona, "perhaps we should go mop up the fountain."

"Ups," Oops, "I forget." Alyona rolls her eyes at the carelessness.

But when we return to the greenhouse, the fountain is clean. The sponge and bucket that cleaned it are on their side outside the gallery leading to the kitchen. Through the spill, the perfect pink prints of a cat emerge and then vanish behind the gallery door. It would be Hello-Kitty-cute if the paws weren't the size of dinner plates.

Taking one step back and then two more, I push Peter with me into a slow retreat.

Alyona remains rigidly still and looks over the conservatory. When her attention passes through the nearest fronds to the glass facing the pool, she asks, "What is this?"

Leisurely watching the yard, Volikov holds the bulky satellite phone to his ear.

Alyona uses her own cell to place a call. She asks, "Where is everyone?" And then answers, "Stay there until—" but the connection drops. "My friends are in tower," she tells me while raising the phone to the glass ceiling. "Reception is running red and green."

Above, on the second landing, the warfare escalates with two quick gunshots: *Bax-babáx! Boom-kaboom!*

Unlike Alyona and I, Volikov doesn't flinch. He simply continues giving instructions into the phone. "Too late for smokejumpers. Send MI-eights and air tankers."

His demeanor is so cool, so relaxed and unconcerned, I'm encouraged to creep forward and join him.

He certainly has an arresting view.

From where we stand, Konstantin's property is divided in two. To the south, the forest unfolds lush and green; to the north, it's charred devastation.

In the pool, Johnny Rotten and a tattooed man sit on opposite sides of the floating picnic table, passing an empty vodka bottle across Elvis's naked body.

On the lawn, Louis Vuitton is carving up the couch cushions with the chef's knife, a tattooed man is singing, the Strongman is crying, and Felix is yelling at his trembling hand.

Then, lest I forget, the Unimog is in the savannah-themed enclosure.

Still holding the phone to his ear, Volikov lights a cigarette with one hand, and tells me, "I watch them drive straight through the fence. First chance at freedom and you know where the lion goes?"

"Where?"

"Right to the kitchen."

My eyes widen.

"*Feh*. Do not worry. The staff are locked inside, safe as little mice."

"And the lion?"

"Last I see him, he was in the foyer admiring the tapestries."

"And the people in the Unimog?"

"If you look past the rammed picnic table, you will see they are napping on the lion's rock."

Just a little farther left of that, someone in a suit is chasing the goat with a banana. "Is that Isaak?"

"Indeed."

Of all the things so far, this strikes me as the most inexplicable. See, Isaak didn't snort Ambien. He was nowhere near the brothers when they railed what they thought was cocaine. And because of his opiate addiction, Isaak doesn't drink, which means Isaak should be as close to sober as anyone here. With or without the banana, there's no good reason for Isaak to be chasing a goat.

"This is the reason I never brought him back to Moscow," Volikov says. "I did it to protect him. He does not have the stomach for real politics. He faints at the sight of blood. Did you know he does not eat meat? He calls himself *vegetarian*."

Volikov says into the phone, "It requires the full force of *Avialesookhrana*." Aerial Forest Protection Service. "I want air tankers and helibuckets. I will stay on line."

The goat that says *Meh*, as all Russian goats do, reaches the fallen fence and quickly hoofs it in search of a gracious space, and Isaak follows with the yellow fruit fully extended.

"But what is he doing?"

"Same thing he does every time we come here: saving the poor creature these degenerates offer the lion. Normally the lion eats big beef patties made in the kitchen—they put a

204

special little herb in it to keep him from ripping his own throat out in boredom—but when Isaak comes to Bereznik, the Bratva always give the lion a meal that can run."

"That is horrible."

"They are thugs. What do you expect?"

"Small decencies?"

"You are sweet. Same reason I cannot take Isaak to Moscow. He has a soft heart. He was already out there trying to lure that stupid creature to safety when they drove through the fence."

In the reflection of the glass, we both watch Alyona take Peter's hand and walk slowly forward to stand beside us. Awestruck by the scene before her, she doesn't think to drop Peter's hand.

Volikov looks to me and I to them and then back to him, and I know he's wondering why I don't have a problem with this.

Looking pointedly at the matching stains on their clothes, Volikov asks Alyona, "Making friends?"

Her expression is cold, murderous steel.

And as I don't particularly want to drive back out into the fire with her tonight, I point their attention east, to Isaak running over the grass, banana before him, calling unheard words into the distance that separates his mouth from the goat's ears. "If he catches it, what does he plan to do with it?"

"As usual, take it home." Shaking his head, he sighs. "No, he would never survive in Moscow."

Chasing the goat into the shooting range, Isaak follows the animal's sharp turn around the activation pillar, but unlike the cloven-hooved ungulate, Isaak slides on the grass. To keep from falling, he grabs the pillar with one hand and allows momentum to swing him 90 degrees back into pursuit, but at the same time he inadvertently triggers the range into life.

The result of Sid Vicious's day of knocking golf balls into the area is instantly felt. As the first trap clangs upright (a smiling Mark Zuckerberg), it zings a fast-moving golf ball at Louis Vuitton by the picnic tables.

The thwack against his back coincides with a shot fired from upstairs.

Vuitton spins to confront his attacker and sees Zuckerberg with a Halo Battle Rifle. Throwing himself to the ground, he belly crawls for the nearest picnic table.

The second spring-loaded trap (Theresa May with an Uzi) rapid-fires three speedballs at two tattooed men.

Upstairs, someone fires down the hall: *Pif! Páf! Pow! Kapow!*

Flipping the picnic table, Vuitton shouts, "Prepare for thunder!" i.e., impact.

The Strongman dives down beside him. Snatching a derringer from an ankle holster, he blindly fires over the table at a fifty-degree angle, sending bullets into the blackened woods.

Isaak doesn't notice. Isaak's only concern is the goat, and the goat's only concern is Isaak. Though, perhaps, by the way he's looking over his shoulder, the goat also has a similar worry to me: where exactly is the lion?

A third trap is triggered, and the entire country of Chechnya rises up with a metallic shwang to hurtle a small array of missiles at the picnic table where Louis Vuitton and the Strongman are pinned down.

Near the sauna, Felix takes notice, and shouts, "What the devil is going on?"

206

And Vuitton calls back, "Bastards are shooting at us."

Squinting into the target range, Felix spends a few seconds focusing his eyes before shouting, "All right, fucker, if that is how you want it." He slaps a tattooed man on the arm, and the two disappear around the side of the house.

At my side, Alyona whispers, "Ready to tell me what was in vodka?"

"Nothing, actually."

"Is a lot of something for nothing."

I look around for Peter and find him slumped to floor, dead asleep, his head resting in the springy new fronds of a fern.

Back outside, an unexpected militant rises in the form of Scarlett Johansson. She comes to the party with a cigar in one hand and dynamite in the other and lobs an errant missile at Johnny Rotten that ricochets off the floating picnic table and rolls to a stop outside the sauna.

But it's Angela Merkel that deals the first real damage. She launches an artillery strike on the conservatory that shatters windows across the entire western front. Glass slices through the vegetation, shearing off leaves before shattering on the tiles.

Covering our heads, Alyona and I cower, but Volikov stands unmoved. He talks calmly into his phone. "Tell the pilot to land in front. If he lands in back, one of these *khuibolisty* will shoot him."

A multilayered insult, khuibolisty means losers, though literally it's dick ballers, like footballers, which is to say dick kickers who involve the balls. Tolstoy would weep.

Upstairs, a single round is fired, *bux, bang,* and the Strongman, peeking over the top of the table, is simultaneously hit between the eyes, *thax, schwack,* by Tommy Hilfiger springing to life with a Stars and Stripes bazooka.

The goat hides behind Johansson, Isaak peels the fruit, and the Strongman crashes to his back.

Still in his underwear, the Fat Man comes screaming and careening out of the Savannah chased by Sid Vicious and the Ken Doll.

The goat startles to Merkel, Isaak follows with the banana, and the Fat Man passes the overturned picnic table— *"Oooyyyaaahhh!" Aaarrrgggghhh!*—on his way for the pool.

Presumably for his own safety, Vuitton tries to take him down with a tackle, but his arms slide down the Fat Man's still heavily oiled body, and he lands with his face in the turf. *Bukh. Thunk.*

With his hands slipping from the Fat Man's ankles, Vuitton struggles to his knees, and Vicious and Ken trip over him.

The Fat Man cannonballs into the pool. The Strongman falls asleep in the grass. And Zuckerberg springs back up to drive a wedge into the stumbling Ken Doll's side.

Ken falls into Vicious who falls onto Vuitton.

Merkel is ratcheting down for another strike, and Vicious is both laughing and swearing, *"Akaka,* blya," *Ahaha,* fuck, when Alyona's phone rings.

Both Volikov and I stretch to look at the screen.

It's Peter.

But Peter is sleeping behind us.

Ripping the phone from her hand, Volikov answers.

A Russian shouts in English, "Where is Konstantin?"

I recognize the voice as Demyan's, and I suspect Alyona does as well, but Volikov doesn't. He does, however, recognize the accent, and he wants to know: "Who is speaking?"

Silence.

"Who is speaking?"

Who is not speaking.

"Who is speaking?"

Nope, who is definitely not speaking. Who has found Peter's option to hold. I know this because Volikov dangles the phone derisively at an angle so we all hear the piercingly high Vitas scream. [1]

Peter mumbles in his sleep, "Two Elements past the Fifth."

And Volikov angrily answers whoever is on the satellite phone, "Of course I am fine. The only way I could shriek like that is with testicle clamps."

While Volikov conveys more pressing information to his associate, I hold my own phone toward the ceiling until the bars settle enough to call Peter's.

Demyan answers, "Hallo?"

"Where are you?"

"In tower."

"Christ's sake, man, get out of there."

"Why? Is more happening?"

The Devil in the Tower... Lord have mercy. "What are you doing up there?"

---

[1] YouTube link: https://www.youtube.com/watch?v=xITSfp-pNeU

"Trying to save fortune. I call fire and forestry service, but I am not Pakhan. Is Konstantin who must call for federal favors, but no one can find him."

"Earlier I heard the cook mention he was in the sauna with a woman. You should come down now and look for him there."

"If I leave tower, I lose reception, and I am holding on four phones with services from here to Moscow."

"Mr. Volikov is sorting out the rescue effort with Mosco—"

"Fuck your mother!"

"Well, okay, but that's a bit... Oh, right: he's a *mother fucker*. Sure. Got it." Not that it matters, the call is dropped.

If Peter were awake, he'd probably say I'd failed in the art of phoneshui, but Volikov simply offers, "The cell towers are burning."

Of course they are. That's what towers do. And if we hope to leave even one tree standing, we really need to get the Devil out of and away from any and all towers.

I consider retrieving him from the tower myself, but on opening the gallery door, I notice the gas-canister assault on the second floor has filled the foyer with an opaque haze of smoke. The tattooed man in Saint John's Ascension is lost in the cloud.

I should probably try to save him.

But I'm unarmed and there's a lion on the loose.

He could even be hiding in the fog.

Or up the stairs... because something is definitely moving down the spiral stairs from the tower. And it's hard to tell on how many feet it will arrive because each foot echoes in the narrow stone passage.

The first footfalls on the marble floor are hurried and end abruptly in an audible *"Ux,"* *Oof,* and a fleshy slap. *Fleaşc.* *Splat.* Flat palms against polished tile sort of splat.

From the mist, someone swears, *"The fuck?"*

"Demyan?"

"Hell did I trip on?"

"A man sleeping in a tapestry. While you're there, maybe drag him out of the smoke."

"Is house on fire?"

"No, that's just a bomb from the floor above."

Silence.

"Demyan?"

"Na khuya?" *For fucking what?* = **Why?** "Why is everyone gone crazy?"

"Now's not the time to agonize. The lion is missing."

"Ex, jób tvojú mat!" Oh, what the fuck! "Rodilá rebjónka: tri nogí, četýre xúja, pjátaja, pizdjónka." Have born a baby: three legs, four dicks, fifth is pussy = **Things** are really messed up.

Beneath an inaudible mumble of continuing obscenities, there's the swoosh of fabric being dragged across the floor. Moments later, at the gallery doors, Demyan materializes with a fistful of tapestry to hurl the cocooned body of a tattooed man into the conservatory.

He points above and says, "I lost all calls. How is Maksim calling?"

"Satellite phone."

211

"Konstantin is in sauna?"

"Maybe."

He stalks out the back of the conservatory to find out.

Upstairs, someone—who I am beginning to suspect is alone—fires another round down the hall, and outside, the Fat Man backstrokes across the pool.

Ken, Vicious, and Vuitton are still pinned down by Chechnya when Hilfiger pops up to zing two balls against the table and one into the stomach of the Fat Man.

Vicious screams at the sky, "Where did *shitstorm* come from?"

To convince the goat how delicious it is, Isaak pretends to eat the banana. *Khrum, khrum. Yum, yum.* And the goat does seem interested, but he's keeping his distance because you can never tell when any of these monkeys might turn.

Halfway to the ground, Zuckerberg glitches out in a spasm of twitches, *klatz-klatz shchyolk, titikity-tik-schwick,* but Johansson springs up to zing a hard one at Johnny Rotten in the pool.

Zvyak. Thwack.

Dazed, he looks around for the source.

Back behind the picnic table, Vuitton shouts, "Gruz-300!" Injured need transport.

Rotten says, "Fuck it," lays his head down on Elvis's belly, and goes to sleep.

Demyan enters the sauna.

Volikov grunts.

Following his gaze to the corner of the house, I see Felix with the RPG.

212

Alyona mutters, "Go´spodi, nyet." Lord, no.

Beside Felix, the Blond with Cornrows holds a second rocket.

Felix squints both eyes to focus on the target range. His steadier hand is on the trigger. His right is on the grip.

Volikov's expression toys with the idea of mild concern.

Vicious makes a run for the house, but Theresa May nails him in the ribs.

For no apparent reason, the Ken Doll howls, "Zába-ága!" Toad-master!

And Felix responds with his favorite toast, "Poye´khali!" Let's do it!

His damaged brain sends a signal to the left hand to pull the trigger, but the transmission crosses to the right as well. Flinging the tube skyward, he launches a missile at the tower.

With the impact, the foundation of the castle shudders.

The goat bolts for the woods.

Isaak drops the banana.

Stones tumble from overhead and smash through the conservatory ceiling, taking glass and steel to the floor. *Babakh! Tararakh! Babakh-trakh! KakaKarash! Crack-a-boom!*

Then Merkel follows with another barrage. *Páf-au-pif-páf. Rat-a-tat-tat.*

The entire western front falls to ruin. The tower only has half a roof.

Volikov considers it with a barely audible *"Errm."* *Hmph.*

Felix says, "Again," and Blond with Cornrows loads the second rocket.

Isaak yells, "You stupid idiot," and stalks past Chechnya.

Volikov steps back.

Alyona and I are already there.

Demyan emerges with Konstantin from the sauna.

Konstantin's brows come together as he questions, "Felix?"

Then his eyes bulge as he cries, *"Nyet!"*

But the neurons have already fired and the signal leaves Felix's brain. It reaches his left hand as Isaak reaches Theresa May. The rocket reaches them both before Felix can answer, *"Uhú?"* Huh?

Where Isaak and Teresa stood, there is nothing. Not even the pink mist of Louisiana hunters killing with tannerite. There's nothing but a trail of smoke exploding in the remains of the western forest.

Looking over his property, Konstantin stumbles where he stands.

The tower is a burning matchstick on the corner of the castle. Half the conservatory is jumbled beneath it. The tables are upturned, and the forest is smoking. Farther west, flames still shoot into the ten o'clock sky and meld with the fireball sunset.

Leaving the leafy green cover of the eastern forest, the lion trots across the grass to throw his front paws over the Pakhan's shoulders and gently maw at his head.

Konstantin drops to his knees.

The lion falls with him. He licks from neck to ear and then chest to eye, raking his tongue over the blood-red skin of the Pakhan.

Somewhere in the smoldering distance, the goat calls out, *"Meh."*

The Aeon

Shuffle the cards right over left, cut the deck three times, and see what the future holds.

In the center is the Sun.

Not to be taken literal. Especially not in Russia where the sun set six months ago and is now only above the horizon for three short hours.

In the Tarot, the Sun is the promise of new life.

Now don't go all sentimental and think baby. No one's pregnant. It's a new life for the dealer. And thank fuck for that.

In the immediate past is the Tower. No shit.

And rather appropriately, the Tower card is singed around the edges from the fire that collapsed the tower roof when Felix shot it with a rocket.

I'd have done this reading sooner, but Konstantin's construction crew only recently dug my cards out of the rubble, and the guards only gave them to me this morning, a morning indistinguishable from night.

Sticking with the whole darkness and ruin theme, back to the Tarot: beside the Tower is the tattered Prince of Coins. Nothing to be surprised about there either. We did see that coming in the first reading.

Below the Sun, in the subconscious mind, are the Three of Swords and the Five of Wands. Water-stained Sorrow and coal-dusted Strife.

Above it, in the conscious mind, are two absolutely filthy swords. Nine cruel stabs and ten ruinous swipes with these things will leave wounds that fester. Being that's my mental state, it's also no news to me.

It's the future I'm hoping for a glimpse of.

Left of the Sun are the Moon and the Wheel of Fortune. The face of the moon is clouded by soot and the wheel is cracked, but their location is heartening.

The Sun and the Moon and the Wheel of Fortune: you could not ask for better.

The future is a circle completed. The future is whole. It's round with life. It's a ball of fire. A guiding light by day and a beacon at night. No one will be lost. No one *could* get lost.

The future is so rich with reward, it makes me smile.

The expression doesn't please Peter.

He asks, "What have you got to be happy about?"

He asks, "Is this the stupid shit your mother taught you?"

He swipes the cards from the table, saying, "Put the filthy things in the trash."

I made the mistake of laying out the cards across from him.

Then I make another mistake with an attempt at levity. "If only my mother had taught me how to steal silver from Tiffany's."

It isn't funny, and he doesn't smile.

But then, the last time I saw Peter smile he had just woken from his rather unexpected 36-hour bender on vodka and hypnotics.

He woke in a state of bliss.

And why not?

Besides being extremely well rested, the last incidents he recalled were taking two Tylenol and watching his fiancée fall down a flight of stairs. The final details his brain was able to commit to memory occurred at Demyan's house, after the respectable consumption of some forty-odd shots of vodka but before his ignoble first meeting with Konstantin; and also before Demyan threatened to tattoo him with his teenage crimes, and before Volikov revealed the kompromat of his corporate crimes, and long before his blundering fiancée involved him in a crime that was still smoking as he opened his eyes.

None of those dangers existed in Peter's mind when he woke in the blue room of Konstantin's castle. A gentle breeze moved the air, and he was still happily oblivious to the reason why. He puzzled briefly over the unfamiliar ceiling and then smiled to see me at his side.

He doesn't smile to see me anymore.

He hasn't smiled since rising from the bed and looking out the shattered windows.

He didn't smile when I said, "You might be wondering..."

He wasn't smiling when he asked, "Where the hell am I?"

When the police confiscated our passports, and Volikov started negotiating with M&H for our release, all remnants of Peter's humor died like the Polar Bear.

Smashed, bashed, dashed, and then utterly burned to ash, I don't think Peter's appreciation for the absurd will ever rise again.

Especially not while we're under house arrest in Moscow. Granted, it's a swank four-bedroom apartment in Patriarshy Ponds sort of arrest, but it's still arrest. It's detention. State custody. Custodial supervision. It's either

M&H signs the contract, supplies the money, and forfeits voting rights, or Peter and his innocent fiancée go to jail.

That's how the negotiators refer to me: the innocent fiancée.

Just a devoted translator.

No idea what was happening.

A victim of circumstance.

Blameless.

But in the six months since we've been held, Peter has learned different.

So has Volikov.

And Demyan.

And Konstantin.

My seven voting shares are long gone.

Which isn't as bad as Konstantin wanting to kill us over the Polar Bear.

Or Demyan's return to jail.

Or that Volikov is the only thing that stands between us and death, and jail, and, not incidentally, the airport.

Not that Peter is in any big hurry to leave. His Finnish, Swedish, and German investors think he's willfully, dutifully staying in Russia. They think he's a hardworking entrepreneur, overseeing the restructuring of Konstantin Imperiya and guaranteeing contracts to buy below market price. Sure, he's hard as hell to reach, but such is to be expected when he's out in the far flung reaches of Berenik's cellular dead zone, or so he tells them.

And anyway, Peter is confident M&H will eventually sign and pay because they're in no position to refuse when Peter knows their business, or, more accurately, their secrets.

"Same exact thing," Peter tells me.

And with a forest the size of Mongolia, or if that's too abstract, the size of Saudi Arabia, or imagine the United Kingdom times five, or a forest as big as the states of Washington, Montana, North Dakota, South Dakota, Wyoming, Idaho, Oregon, and Utah combined, with a forest that size, the fire did little more than swallow Boise.

As Peter likes to say, "The Russian timber industry is a drunk virgin about to be fucked by the football team."

Peter wants to be captain, but for now he's content to still be in the starting lineup.

You didn't actually think any of the players in this game were nice, did you?

We should all be long past such illusions by now.

There's no one to root for here. Go home. Leave your memorabilia in the trash by the doors. Or throw it on the ground. Environmental concerns are not paramount.

"Earth first," as Peter says. "We'll gang rape the other planets later."

And on Earth, Russia is the girl everyone wants to date. She has quick access to Europe and Asia, and coming-of-age soon is her best-friend-forever the Arctic.

"Now the Arctic is the wedding we've all been waiting for," Peter says. "Before the reception is even over, the bride's white dress will be torn from her body."

In preparation, Peter is using the time to learn Cyrillic.

And teaching him is the only use he has for me now. I'm trying my best to thwart his success and retain value, but he's a fast learner when motivated.

What's driving him at the moment is the new timber contract, and a complete lack of trust in me.

He will *never* trust another translator again.

"Ever," he adds. "In fact, make that to infinity."

I've liberated him.

Sometimes the freedom even earns me a few caustic words of gratitude. "I am one hundred percent thankful we met. *Really, I am.*"

On the Wi-Fi disabled laptop provided by the State, he reads the new agreement between Konstantin Imperiya and M&H Enterprise in the original Cyrillic.

Frowning, he swivels the laptop to face me and frenetically runs the cursor over the passage: В случае мокрое дело, акции, принадлежащие совету директоров, передаются назначенным кандидатам.

With difficulty, he reads aloud, "In case of..."—*мокрое дело*—"...shares held by the board of directors will pass to designated candidates."

He highlights the unknown words: *Мокрое дело.*

"Mokroye delo," I say. "It means wet work." But that's literal. In context of what he's reading, it's murder.

If we weren't in a digital black hole, he'd be able to look it up online, but we have no phone, no broadband, no satellite. We're allowed no communication with the outside world without prior authorization from the warden, which is to say Volikov, and because Volikov is in hiding from Konstantin, the prior part of that authorization makes the whole thing moot.

The only time Peter talks with his investors is when I give the guards Bitcoin and they give Peter their phones.

Still, better than Demyan has it.

An admirable thief in law in every way, he lived the code inked on his skin—vor vora kroyet, a thief covers another thief—and took whatever blame there was to be taken for his brothers.

Once more before the courts, he assumed guilt for destruction of property, arson, and the only illegal firearm found on the property: the RPG that accidentally killed Isaak.

Yes, that's right: *accidentally.*

It was all an unfortunate accident. I made a sworn statement saying as much. As did Felix, and Konstantin, and every other witness.

Except Volikov.

Volikov isn't the sort of man to make statements that require signatures.

The rest of us—no matter what we saw or actually remembered—swore Demyan had no idea Isaak was in the shooting range. What sort of lunatic would be?

The special investigator wanted to know, "What sort of lunatic fires at targets with an RPG?"

And we all pointed at Demyan. He's the sort. Have you seen his tattoos? A veritable outlaw with no respect for convention. Take him away.

It's the way he wanted it.

For Felix, Demyan accepted the charge of *common corpus delicti*, more-or-less the equivalent of involuntary manslaughter.

It's not all bad. He's getting a promotion in the guild and stars tattooed on his shoulders, then hopefully, when he's released in six years, he'll quickly overthrow Konstantin to become Pakhan. An outcome that would be ideal for Peter and me. (Well, honestly, mostly just me.)

Until then, we're relying on Volikov for protection, which is far from ideal as both Konstantin and Demyan want him dead. And both for the same reason: it's only for Volikov's insistence that someone be held accountable for Isaak's death that Demyan is in jail.

Only the Devil might imagine what shades of red Demyan is seeing now, but I bet it was pretty close to oxblood his first night in jail. Before the family could even welcome him home, he'd organized six thieves on motorbikes to shoot up Volikov's car.

True, the objective was to shoot up the car *and* Volikov, but Volikov's car—from the armor in the panels to the glass in the windows and right down to the honeycomb tires—is bullet resistant.

Escaping with his life, Volikov doubled his guard.

During those first tumultuous months, Konstantin also proved he was still red in tooth and claw.

With no idea Demyan was after his crown, and with retribution his right as a disrespected Pakhan, Konstantin orchestrated a show of revenge Moscow hadn't seen since the 90s.

It started when Volikov's brand new bullet-resistant car exploded on a city street. I'm told by the guards that shredded metal and upholstery draped the power lines for weeks, and the honeycomb tires remain four black puddles on the pavement.

They tell me his home waterline was poisoned while he slept, and his private club torched while he ate.

Odorless methane filled his office and killed five in an explosion the news reported as a gas leak.

Finally, Volikov went to ground, but not before trebling both his and our guard.

Our guard because of our part in the Polar Bear's demise.

Did you think we could drag a bleeding body out of the castle and stuff it in a Studebaker shitting rainbows without anyone noticing?

Relax. If you did, I wouldn't fault you for it. *I* thought it was possible. But I also thought our luck would return when we ditched the corpse and the numbers in play stopped being four and eight and changed to three and nine. Didn't help a bit in the end.

Maybe it was the numbers, but in retrospect, I think the problem was not thinking big enough. The situation required blue-sky action, column-shaking leadership, 360-degree innovation. *Everyone* in the house should have been drugged, from the brothers to the staff to the women hired for the weekend.

In the bedrooms on the second and third floors, Alyona's friends—entirely too sober and aware—noticed her gaily driving off with the two Americans and the bloody remains of a Bratva.

And the sorority of whores has no code of ethics such as the thieves in law.

Alyona sold herself to Konstantin and then her friends sold her again.

Now, with both Konstantin and Volikov gunning for her, Alyona is also in hiding.

Peter doesn't care because Peter doesn't know who the hell Alyona is. He's only heard of her through me, and nothing I say can be trusted.

"For all I know," he says, "this woman doesn't exist." And further, all he wants to know is, "What the fuck do wet works have to do with who gets control of the board?"

He rereads the contract on the screen. "In the case of wet work, shares held by the board of directors will pass to designated candidates."

Slamming closed the laptop, his voice rises with irritation. "What the hell are we talking here? Plumbing? If the toilet backs up, do we lose our shares?"

"It's a euphemism from Bureau Thirteen of the KGB, which was also informally known as the Department of Wet Affairs."

"Sex?"

"Well, they did enjoy playful capital punishment and strict executions, but their true passion was public assassinations."

Three quick blinks and an angry scowl later, he demands clarification, "Wet for spilling blood?"

"I suspect in the context of the agreement, it would cover all contract kills, regardless of spillage."

"Think this is funny?"

"Just pointing out it's not all sniper rifles and razor wire. Russians love their radioactive poisons, as well."

"Sweet fucketty fuck, is this actually the sort of shit Russians have to cover in a contract?"

226

"Did you actually bring us here without knowing that?"

Peter opens the laptop again. Glaring at the screen as though hate alone might turn Cyrillic into English, he demands, "Have you read this?"

"How could I when you won't let me near it?"

Shoving the laptop across the table, he orders, "Read it and tell me what fuckery I've missed. And don't fuck with me, Sibyl. I goddamn mean it, just tell me what it says."

"All of it?"

"The shit between the lines. The tricky bits. You'll recognize it. That's the language you speak."

Fair enough. But have you noticed someone isn't speaking jargon? House arrest with a person you loathe can have such effects. Especially in those early months when one of you is coming off a decade of pills, and the other offers motivation in the form of "Dive deep to deep six the pain point," and "Winners never quit, quitters never win," and the one that finally broke me: "Mind over matter. Stop minding and it won't matter." Never mind the full-abstinence abrupt-withdrawal let-me-tell-you-what-I-really-think fits of honesty, it's the insomnia, it's Russia in winter, sunset at noon, and the promise of perpetual midnight with someone who says, "Don't watch the clock. Do what it does: keep ticking," that truly gets one talking. I don't think I spared him a single detail.

By month three, Peter had been cured of artifice, me of pills, and each of the other.

At this point in our forced cohabitation, nothing either of us says can hurt, and as the only thing I've not read twice in the house is the instructions on the shampoo bottle, I'm more than a little pleased to read the contract.

It's a fairly straightforward ass beating of Morris & Hugo.

They pay to rebuild the sawmill for which they receive the fuck-all rights and profits of ordinary shareholders in a private Russian company.

Under the wet work clause, Isaak's shares are appointed to Volikov.

Of interest, Azart is still in the game for ten percent.

With Demyan in jail, I suspect Felix might also be a secret board member of the offshore company, and if they too had a wet work clause, and assuming all three thieves in law within the Zomanov Bratva, excluding Konstantin himself, were in collusion, then the Polar Bear's shares were returned to Azart (because Alyona definitely did some wet work on him [Christ, how I wish I could still blame my humor on the drugs]).

The new contract gives Konstantin twenty-one shares and thirty percent of the board against Volikov's thirty shares and fifty percent. Demyan's ten shares and twenty-percent control allows him to swing the votes. The arrangement makes the wet work clause a veritable gold-and-vellum invitation to kill. Let's make it a surprise: No RSVP required.

Morris & Hugo have thirty-nine shares, but no voting rights, no place on the board, no purpose other than investment for ransom.

"There's no mention of the paper mill," I say.

"It's off."

"They've dropped the paper mill?"

"Under those terms, there's no incentive."

But what an opening.

228

For the first time in months, I get a glimpse of the Sun. I see the Wheel of Fortune shining under the rays of the noon Sun, and glowing by the light of a full Moon

I see hope. I see prosperity. I see the future.

The Sun is the promise of a new beginning.

The Moon is me, my home, my fate, my life, safe in the sky.

And the Wheel of Fortune turns. It's always turning.

Mind you, it's not always good with the wheel. But my luck has been on the downward spin, so the only way for it to go is up. And it doesn't have to turn much to elevate the likes of me. See, the ups and downs of everyone's life depend on the size of the wheel.

Great fortunes rise on a great wheel. The ascent is dizzying, the view from the top glorious, but the fall is sickening, the circle is huge, and it's easy to get crushed at the bottom.

Small lives: small turns. Little fortunes: little loss.

Big lives: big turns. Colossal fortunes: colossal crash.

Konstantin, Volikov, Morris, and Hugo are all in the midst of a terrifying dive.

It's the size of the wheel.

Peter is scrambling not to be crushed by the weight of it.

My life is small, so the fall didn't hurt.

In fact, I'm already in line for another go.

There's no minimum height to ride. It's open all night. It turns in all weather. You too hold a ticket, and you're riding with us whether you like it or not.

It's not a threat, it's a journey.

Let me tell your fortune.

You enter the fair as a Fool. You walk under the Sun and the Star and the Moon. You dine with Emperors and study with Hierophants. You leave Lovers like Hanged Men scattered across the Universe. You play with the Magus and fall from the Tower. You race in the Chariot to hide from Death and become a Hermit. The Empress lures you out with love, then the Priestess spikes your drink. You're taken by the Devil. You make Art. You Lust. You Adjust. You enter the Aeon, and there, at the end, a stranger tells your Fortune.

Lightning Source UK Ltd.
Milton Keynes UK
UKHW051305190622
404623UK00006B/145

9 781370 068876